An Evening With Champions

Sam Zuckert

KEEP IT GOING LOUDER PRESS

ISBN: 979-8-218-48455-2
First Printing, 2024

Cover design by Anni Zuckert

keepitgoinglouderplease@gmail.com

2 8 1 3 3 0 8 0 0 4

For Bubbie and Zadie

AN EVENING WITH CHAMPIONS

Contents

1

Mr. Fluffington, DDS

From the moment Ashley first saw him, she knew Mr. Fluffington was going to be a dentist. It was two weeks after they moved to Medford, Papa George took Ashley to Dog Rescue Boston and told her to not make him regret his decision. Ashley practically floated down the aisle of cages, her eyes darting from terrier to hound to collie to schnauzer. They were all so cute! There was a small brown sheepdog with the saddest eyes, a squat bulldog that must have had double or triple asthma, and a retriever that looked majestic enough to saddle up and ride off into the sunset. She wanted them all, but when she came to the end of the row and saw Mr. Fluffington, all the other dogs vanished from her mind.

He was a black labradoodle with a shock of white around his torso that looked like a perfectly bespoke lab coat. She stood in front of Mr. Fluffington's cage and when they locked eyes, it felt like he already knew everything about her. He flashed his dainty canines at Ashley and playfully tapped his paws against the cage. He was the one. She called over Papa George and he asked if she was sure, because they weren't getting another one anytime soon. She had never been more sure of anything in her life.

The staff let Mr. Fluffington out of his cage and when he sauntered up to Ashley, she smiled so wide that Papa George saw her teeth for the first time in months. She snapped her lips closed as soon as she felt the air on her gums, but when Mr. Fluffington started licking her neck and nuzzling into her shoulder, her self-consciousness disappeared and her smile crept back open. Mr. Fluffington was going to become the best dentist the world had ever seen.

———

Three months earlier, Papa George sat Ashley down at the kitchen table in their cramped apartment and told her that they would be moving to Massachusetts. Their third move in two years. She would have to start *another* new school for 5th grade.

Papa George had picked her up from soccer practice and seemed strangely quiet on the ride home. He usually would show her pictures of a necklace or a set of earrings he was working on at the shop, but today he was withdrawn. Ashley found it a bit odd, but didn't think much of it until they got home and he had her favorite dinner ready on the stove. Something was wrong. She ran her tongue over her braces, feeling each bracket and wire, and steeled herself for what was coming. He told her that he found a full-time job at a jewelry shop outside of Boston, and they would be able to afford a nice house and a car and everything would be much better.

After he finished his speech, he put his hand on her shoulder and said, "Ashley, I know this has been hard on you, but this one is for real." That's what he said when they left Illinois the first time too. William, his "mentor", wanted them to come live with him in Kansas City and it was a really good opportunity for them. Six months later, they were back in Illinois.

While they ate, Papa George kept glancing over at Ashley, preparing himself for her to fight back and plead for them not to move. She had not taken the news well for the last two moves, and Ashley figured that the next time he had to give her bad news he would do it at home to minimize the chance of any outburst. Truthfully, she was miserable in this far-flung Chicago suburb, a move could be a good chance for a new start. But she didn't need to let Papa George know that. He felt bad and that was golden, she wasn't going to give it up for nothing.

After a few more bites, Ashley broke the silence. "Papa George, can we get ice cream after dinner?"

"Sure baby, after we do the dishes."

"Two scoops?"

"Have you cleaned your braces every night this week?"

"I think."

"We'll see." Locked and loaded. She was going to get a goddamn dog.

Ashley cleaned the table while Papa George did the dishes, and after the apartment was made tidy and neat, they put on their shoes and walked out to the ice cream parlor. It was a warm June night, a dozen other families waited in line while the teenagers behind the counter took turns serving scoops. Ashley had been planning for months, but in her head she always imagined it being a spur of the moment thing. Having the time to pick her moment was a welcome surprise. She waited for them to get about halfway through the line, six families in front of them, four behind. A few of the other kids in line went to her school, but none of them were in her grade. Perfect.

She started with a sniffle. Soft, subtle, didn't want to draw much attention to herself at first. Let it build. When the line moved and Papa George took a step forward, she remained in place. He tapped her arm and told her to step forward, that's when she flipped the switch.

"I don't want to move again!"

"Ashley, honey…"

"Papaaa Geoooooorge, I don't want to move again!!!"

"Honey, not here, please."

Just like she practiced in her room, Ashley let her legs turn to jelly and she flopped to the ground. She let her arm land first, smacking her hand onto the linoleum tiles for dramatic effect. Everyone in the store turned to look at the two of them. Que waterworks.

"We just moved last year!" Sob. "And now we have to move again?!" Sob sob. "And you won't even get me a puppy!" Sob sob sob sob sob sob sob sob.

"Please, Ashley…"

"I know you haven't found a job here, but I'm sure if you keep trying you can find one!" She knew it was a low blow, but this wasn't hopscotch, there was a dog on the line. "I won't have any friends! You said you would think about getting a puppy last time we moved but we never did!" Tears tears, sob sob, sniffle sniffle sniffle sniffle.

"We talked about this…"

"Please please pleeeeeeeease! Can we at least get a puppy so I have ONE friend when we move?!"

By this point the teenagers had stopped scooping and the line had stopped moving and everyone watched as Papa George knelt over Ashley, still splayed out on the floor.

"Okay, we can get a dog."

"We can?" Ashley threw in a few more sniffles, just for insurance.

Papa George leaned closer to her and hissed, "Yes, we can get a dog when we move, just stand up and stop making a scene *right now*." Ashley slowly stood up, brushed the dust from her shirt, and wiped the tears from her eyes. If she knew it was going to be that easy, she would have asked for a new bike too.

— — —

On the ride home from the rescue shelter, Ashley and Mr. Fluffington started digging into the important stuff. She quizzed him about his research experience and specialty interests. All his answers were thoughtful and inspiring. His enthusiasm for oral medicine was contagious! As they drove, Papa George turned half-way around and said, "Ashley, you know having a dog is a lot of responsibility."

"Ugh, yes Papa George!" Of course it would be a lot of responsibility, she had to prepare him to start dental school in the fall!

"You're going to have to feed him and wash him and walk him three or four times a day. I'll help, but he's your dog so he's your–"

"He's my responsibility, I know!"

Ashley could see Papa George roll his eyes in the rearview mirror, he didn't even know the half of it. She learned that Mr. Fluffington had a solid academic resume, but he hadn't finished all his prerequisites, so they would need to hit the books hard to make sure he was ready for classes to start in the fall.

When they got home, Papa George opened the trunk and looked at Ashley and looked at the trunk and looked at Ashley and said, "I'll get all the food and stuff, you two go have fun." Ashley shot out of the car with Mr. Fluffington and they frolicked around the neighborhood until they could frolic no more. Once the sun started to set, Papa George shouted out at them from the porch to come get ready for dinner. They came running inside, and once they got washed up, she plopped down at the table, still grinning from ear to ear. Mr. Fluffington climbed onto her lap and rested his head on Ashley's lap as Ashley pet his head.

She looked down and said, "Hope you had fun today Mr. Fluffington, because tomorrow, our work begins." Mr. Fluffington looked up at her and nodded approvingly, then lay his head back down and softly panted till he caught his breath.

—— —— ——

The whole next week, Ashley was happy as a clam. She and Mr. Fluffington spent every waking hour together going on long walks, talking about patient care theory, and brushing their teeth with extraordinary care. They did the dental school prerequisite diagnostics tests and Mr. Fluffington was okay on biology and physics, but woefully unprepared in chemistry. He hadn't even taken a single course that covered organic topics! She ordered the recommended books online, and was hoping to get to work right away when they arrived, but

Papa George opened the package before she could get to it and did not look happy when he arrived in her doorway holding them.

"Ashley, what is this?"

"It's an Organic Chemistry textbook, Mr. Fluffington needs it to study so he can pass his prerequisite subjects tests."

"Excuse me?"

"For school! Classes start on September–"

"Ash, what are you talking about?"

Ashley took a deep breath. She knew she was going to have to tell Papa George eventually about Mr. Fluffington enrolling in dental school, but she just figured if she put it off until after he started, then it would be easier to explain.

"Papa George, Mr. Fluffington is going to be a dentist."

"What?"

"He's going to dental school! We found an online program that works perfect with his schedule, and as long as he passes the prerequisite tests, he can do the first two years online and then finish up with an in-person clinic placement in Boston!"

Papa George looked confused. And concerned. And maybe a little angry? Sometimes it was hard for Ashley to tell. He was always so boxed in with his emotions, she kinda wished that Mr. Fluffington wanted to be a psychologist so he could help Papa George, but you can't choose your dog's passion. She was sure there were more than enough competent psychologists around Boston, but how to convince Papa George to go to one? That was the main challenge. She got so lost in her train of thought that she didn't hear Papa George calling out to her until he raised his voice.

"Ashley! Dental School?! What are you talking about? Is that what you've been doing in your room all these days? Have you been reading textbooks to the dog?!"

"Papa George, his name is Mr. Fluffington, and I don't think you understand, I–"

"What's there to understand?! A dog can't go to dental school, that's insane!"

"But that's his passion! He told me he's always wanted to be a dentist!"

"Ashley, I know moving is hard, but you need to go outside and make some friends or you're going to be miserable once school starts."

"But Mr. Fluffington needs my help–"

"I met a nice woman at the grocery store who said she had a daughter your age, I didn't want to do this, but tomorrow you *will* go over to their house and make friends with her."

"If he doesn't start studying chemistry then he'll be way behind before classes even start!"

"I know the kids at your last school were mean, but if you don't put yourself out there, then it will be just as bad at this one."

"But–"

"I'm calling her right now. You're going over to their house tomorrow and that's final." Ashley looked down at Mr. Fluffington, he pawed at her leg to tell her that they had to pick their battles, and this was not one they needed to win.

"Okay."

"Thank you Ashley, I appreciate your being mature about this."

The next day, Papa George dropped Ashley off at Kacey O'Connor's house at 1pm. They had a bland and inoffensive afternoon. Kacey showed her all her toys and they played with her pet turtle, Winona. When Ashley got hungry they rummaged through Kacey's cabinets and got some snacks. Ashley asked if they had any cheese crackers, Kacey looked down at the ground.

"We don't have any dairy in the house, I'm really allergic."

"Like you're lactose intolerant?"

"Kinda, I just kinda throw up a lot."

"Gross."

"I know." They settled on peanut butter sandwiches and after a bit of chewing, Ashley saw Kacey looking at her teeth. She pursed her lips but she could tell Kacey was curious. "Does it hurt to eat with your braces?"

"Sometimes. Usually not."

"My brother has braces. My mom says I'll probably need them when I'm older."

"Maybe."

"Not a lot of kids our age have them yet."

"Yeah, I guess."

They finished the rest of their sandwiches in silence. After snack time they did some coloring outside, then jumped on her trampoline, and at 4pm exactly she said goodbye and sat in front of the house until Papa George picked her up. "See? Wasn't that fun?" He asked. She nodded politely and even thanked him for setting it up. She figured it couldn't hurt to start collecting some brownie points. For the rest of the ride she looked out the window and started planning how Mr. Fluffington would make up for the study time they lost that day.

— — —

Once the school year started, Ashley and Mr. Fluffington settled into a comfortable rhythm. They would wake up and go over flashcards in the morning before breakfast. Then, after they ate, Papa George would drive Ashley to school and Mr. Fluffington would stay at home for independent study.

Ashley mostly kept to herself throughout the school day. She found that if she sat at her desk, did her work, and didn't make a fuss, the teachers would let her be and the other students would steer clear. At recess she sat at one of the picnic tables and reviewed notes from the material that she and Mr. Fluffington were working on. During the anatomy unit, she would color in diagrams of teeth, highlighting the enamel and retracing the roots. When they reached physiology, she cut out pictures of streptococcus bacteria to go with the dental papilla.

Every once in a while she would look up and see the other kids running around the playground, kicking a soccer ball or playing tag on the jungle gym. She remembered when she would have loved nothing more than to go chase around a ball with her classmates, but she hadn't felt that urge since two moves ago when they still lived in Kansas. It had all happened so fast, she had never even touched a soccer ball until William suggested to Papa George that he sign her up for a team. The first time she laced up her brand new cleats and kicked a ball as hard as she could, she felt a peculiar thrill, and was obsessed from that day on. She would get so excited to play soccer at recess that she would jitter at her desk and was a frequent visitor to her classroom's Calm-Down Corner. Her teacher always made her stand at the back of the line to go outside, but even that couldn't dampen her spirits, because as soon as she got onto the field she would sprint so hard it felt like she was going to lift off the ground and start flying.

She played with joyous abandon, chasing after every pass and throwing her feet at any ball that got off the ground. The boys had teased her at the start of the year, but once they saw her play, they developed a begrudging respect.

Then one day, everything changed. It started out like any other day; math and reading in the morning, arts class before lunch, out to the fields at recess. The sky was clear and calm, a mild fall afternoon, perfect to run around. And run they did, up and down, back and forth, non-stop for twenty-seven minutes until a teacher blew a whistle and yelled, "Two minutes left! Two minutes left till line-up!" The ball rolled into the middle of the field as everyone stopped to listen. When the announcement ended, Ashley locked eyes with Cameron, a boy on the other team, and they both started sprinting to the ball. He got there first and took a hard turn towards the goal. Ashley chased after, at first a step behind him, but quickly catching up. Cameron angled towards the left edge of the goal, which should have been an easy stop for their goalie, but Ashley checked his position and saw that he was picking his nose and playing with a frog that had hopped onto the field. She would have to make the stop herself.

Ashley dropped her head and dug her feet hard into the dirt. Cameron could dribble well but was known on the playground for having a wild shot, considering her goalie was mostly indisposed, Ashley guessed he was going to try and dribble it all the way. She took two more big strides and then lunged for the ball, but as she attacked, her foot landed wrong and she tumbled forward, straight towards the goalpost. She held out her arms, trying to keep her balance, but her body was too far ahead of her legs and she could feel gravity dragging her down. She looked up and her face slammed into the goalpost with a deep crunch.

The next thing she remembered was lying on the ground with the whole grade standing over her. A teacher shoved through the crowd and yelled, "Back up BACK UP! Everyone!"

She spent the rest of the day drifting in and out of consciousness, each time in a new, disorientation location. First in the nurse's office, then an ambulance, then a dental chair. Papa George had rushed over when the school called him, and he held her hand as the dentist worked. Her two front teeth had been knocked back almost a full inch. The surgery to move them back into place was relatively simple, but because her mouth was still growing she would need to wear braces for a few years to make sure they stayed in place.

When she returned to school a few days later, everyone was very kind to her, but it felt like a distance had emerged. Like she wasn't the same person they had been playing soccer with a few days ago. Like she had changed.

That first month was excruciating. The dentist said she wasn't allowed to play sports so she just sat and watched. The dull pain from the braces pulling on her teeth made it hard to concentrate on anything else. She tried reading, coloring, smacking sticks against her legs, but nothing helped. After the month was up, she and Papa George went to the store and got a dozen mouthguards so she would always have one nearby. But when she went back onto the field for the first time, her lips bulging with the soft plastic covering her teeth, something felt off. Whenever she had the ball the other team gave her plenty of space and whenever she pressured on defense, they would pretty much just give her the ball. When she put her bright blue mouthguard in between her teeth it felt like she was waving a flag that said *go easy on me.*

The rest of the year went by in a haze. Looking back, she remembered that Pappa George and William started getting in fights, how he started spending whole nights locked in his room working on his jewelry. But at the time, it barely even registered with her. It was like some show that was on a TV way in the distance, she could see the outline of shapes and heard the vague tone of the sounds, but all of it blurred together. When Papa George told her in March that they were moving back to Illinois, she felt nothing.

The pity the kids showed her in Kansas was bad, but at least they knew who she was before the accident. Back in Illinois, they moved to some stupid suburb a hundred-thousand miles away from where they used to live in the city and it was the middle of the year, so when Papa George dropped her off for her first day at the new school, it felt like he had punted her right into the deep end. All the other kids saw was her clunky braces and the goofy mouthguard she had to wear in gym class and at recess. No one else in the elementary school had braces, so she was a target. They called her brace-face, metal-mouth, tinsel-teeth, carbon-canine, glassy-gummy, bionic-bicuspid, ten-ton-tin-tongue, cheesegrater, and more. Ashley was used to letting her aggression out on the field, but she wasn't able to let loose like she could before. She hesitated before running after a ball, thought-twice before going for a header. Sure, she was quick and had a few moves, but without her old ferocity, she was middle of the pack at best. She might as well be sitting on the grass playing with frogs.

So when she lugged the dental textbooks out to recess everyday and caught a glimpse of the soccer game from afar, she felt like she was looking back in time. A life she once lived but was no longer able to grasp. After a few moments, she would look back down at Mr. Fluffington's course notes and put the field out of her mind. No sense dwelling on the past. They had midterms to study for.

— — —

When Ashley got home from school, she would take Mr. Fluffington out for a walk around the block. They both had busy days, so it was nice to clear their minds with a stroll and some idle chit-chat. Papa George didn't get home from work until right before dinnertime, so once they got back, they would hit the books. Ashley would pull out the lesson organizer and they would review the previous day's content, then they would log on to the online platform and watch the pre-recorded lectures. Ashley would take notes for Mr. Fluffington so he could concentrate fully on absorbing the new material. Then they would work through that day's homework together, clicking on multiple choice bubbles for the pop quizzes and typing in text for free response questions. After they were finished with the daily lessons and assignments, Ashley and Mr. Fluffington would do one last review, then Ashley would file away the notes in her organizer and they would head downstairs for dinner.

Papa George would always ask how her day was, and Ashley would have loved to tell him all about microbiopic functions and lateral incisors, but she was so tired after a full day at school and a full afternoon studying with Mr. Fluffington that she usually just grunted some platitudes and went back to eating.

One day in October, Papa George struck a different tone. "Honey, can I ask you something?"

"What?"

"Ms. Jacobson called today."

"Okay."

"She says you've been great in class, a perfectly delightful student…but she's noticed that you haven't really made any friends and you spend all recess writing in your notebook."

"I have some friends."

"Who?"

"Kacey."

"I asked about Kacey, Ms. Jacobson said she hasn't seen you two playing together outside of class groups."

"Maybe she's not watching"

"Ashley."

"What?"

"Why don't you play with the other kids during recess?"

"I have work to do."

"What work?"

"For school."

"Ms. Jacobson told me that your notebook is filled with doodles of teeth."

"So?"

"Are you still pretending that Mr. Fluffington is in dental school?"

"No."

"Ashley…"

"I'm not pretending! He *is* in dental school!"

Papa George pinched the top of his nose with his right hand. "I know moving has been hard on you, but you can't keep hiding from the world behind make believe."

"I'm not making anything up!"

Ashley could feel her body start to tense and Papa George's voice fade into a low whine. She had friends! Or she used to at least, before they started moving every year. If Papa George could ever hold down a job long enough to keep them in one place, maybe he wouldn't have to set her up on lame play dates so he could feel better about himself as a dad. But here we were, third school in three years, who knows how many more. Unlike Papa George, Mr. Fluffington had a long-term plan, and it was up to her to help him accomplish it.

Ashley shoved herself away from the table and stormed off to her room. Mr. Fluffington trotted after her, and once he passed through the threshold, she slammed the door closed. Sitting with her back against the door, tears started budding in her eyes. Mr. Fluffinton crawled into her lap and nuzzled his head against her arms. She leaned down to kiss him on the head and as she gently pet him she whispered into his ear, "Don't listen to Papa George, you're going to be an amazing dentist and we're going to set up a nice office in one of those cute little buildings that looks like a person's house, and all the kids are going to want to come to you to clean their teeth and fix their braces, and you're going to make a lot of money, and we're going to buy a house and live there forever. You'll be the best dentist ever." Mr. Fluffington looked up at Ashley and nodded in agreement.

— — —

Ashley and Papa George settled into a cold war. He would make offhand comments about Mr. Fluffington's schooling and try and goad Ashley into making new friends, Ashley would brush him off and they would leave it at that. She was relieved when Papa George found a districation. He made a new friend named Blake, and by December they were spending almost every night together. It was perfect, not only because Papa George seemed happy, but because Blake was getting Papa George out of the house and left Ashley and Mr. Fluffington all alone to focus on their studies.

Sometimes Papa George and Blake would have sleepovers, and in the mornings, Blake was always friendly and kind. He would ask Ashley about school and Mr. Fluffington, and when she told him about his progress in dental school, Blake was fascinated. She even overheard him gushing to Papa George about her. He said that Mr. Fluffington becoming a dentist was tremendous camp and Papa George should be proud of Ashley's creativity. She thought he might have been a little confused, because Mr. Fluffington was in dental school not summer camp, but she was glad he noticed the thought she put into decorating and organizing the binders and notebooks. She liked Blake.

But at the end of January, the atmosphere at home started to change. Papa George was acting even more distant than normal and Blake was not as chatty with her as he was before. Ashley hoped that he and Papa George weren't fighting, this was the longest Papa George's friends had ever stuck around, and she remembered how glum Papa George had been when his last friend stopped spending time with him. One night when Blake and Papa George were in his room, she crept up next to the door and placed her ear against the wood. She could hear them whisper-yelling.

"Blake, we just moved here, and you see how hard it is for Ashley to adjust. She still hasn't made any real friends."

"George, this could be my big break. I need to take this chance. *We* need to take this chance. I'm sure there are a million jewelry shops out there you can work for."

"But it's not even a full-time role! You only have a few lines…"

"I only have a few lines *to start*. Once they see the energy I bring, they'll build up my character. I know it."

"What if you just go for the start and–"

"George, I can't fly back and forth from LA every weekend, I need to be there, on call, all day every day. That's how it works."

Ashley stepped back from the door. Los Angeles?! Another move…and so soon? It hadn't even been a full school year. She paced back and forth in the hallways collecting her thoughts.

She liked it in Medford, better than Assville, Illinois at least, but California could be the perfect place for Mr. Fluffington to set up his practice. Sure, the dental schools weren't as good out there, but once he was licensed and certified, there would surely be no shortage of potential patients to help. If he became popular enough, maybe they would even make a reality show about him! Mr. Fluffington: The Star. She could see it now. Only issue was, they had already confirmed with the dental school that Mr. Fluffington would be doing his in-person clinic internship this summer at University Dental in Boston and Mr. Fluffington had to complete two more classes before he could start. The original plan had been to finish the two classes in May and start the internship in June, but if they really busted their humps, they could finish in February and start the internship in the spring semester. It could work. She had been exchanging emails with the Internship Coordinator just that week, she would see if she could set up a meeting to expedite the timeline.

———

Ashley got the meeting scheduled for later that week, and in the meantime, they started working overtime to get through the two required classes. Three hours studying every night instead of just two, and on the weekend they got up super early for an all-day study-a-thon. It was tough, after the long days cramming Oral Pathology and Histology their brains were fried. But it all felt worth it at the end of each night when they would cuddle up in bed, knowing that they were that much closer to Mr. Fluffington becoming a dentist.

During school, Ashley could hardly focus on what Ms. Jacobson was teaching. Her mind would jump from lesson scheduling to internship logistics and back again. More than once, when Ms. Jacobson called on her in class, Ashley had no idea what was going on and just sat there in silence till Ms. Jacobson moved on. It was too cold for outdoor recess, so her class was banished to the gym after lunch, and Ashley would settle into one of the corners to organize Mr. Fluffington's study material for the day. A few days before the meeting, she was particularly frazzled. Her papers were a mess and when she opened her binder they exploded out all over the gym floor. She rushed to pick them up and as she was grabbing them, another pair of hands reached down to help out. It was Kacey.

"Oh, hi Kacey."

"Do you need some help?"

"Umm, sure, yes. Thank you! It's been a long week. I was trying to get my papers and–"

"What are all these papers for?"

"What?"

"I see you every day with your big binder, making drawings or something. What do you do with all these?"

"It's for my dog, he's studying to be a dentist."

"Cool! Like a dentist for other dogs?"

"No, a dentist for humans. Dentists for dogs go to veterinary school, Mr. Fluffington goes to a real dental school."

"Oh, okay. Can I see?"

Ashley looked at Kacey and scrunched her face. Had Papa George asked Kacey to spy on her? Why was she so interested? But after a few moments, Kacey's eyes twinkled, and Ashley decided she was harmless. "Sure, these are his study guides and here are the notes we take for each lecture." She flipped through some of the paper. "And these are the anatomy drawings."

"Whoa, you made all these?"

"Me and Mr. Fluffington did, yes."

"Wow, that's cool."

"Yes…thanks. Thanks. It is!"

"You remember my turtle Winona? I wonder what she could be."

"Anything she puts her mind to."

For the rest of the week, Kacey joined Ashley at recess and while Ashley was working on Mr. Fluffington's dental work, Kacey dreamed up all kinds of careers for Winona. It was nice to have someone to share markers with and laugh about the silly games the other kids were playing. It was nice to have someone to trust. She even brought extra snacks to share with Kacey; no dairy, she remembered, lest Kacey upchuck all over her notes.

Ashley told Kacey all about the meeting she had with the Internship Coordinator at University Dental. They were going to get a tour of the facilities and then Ashley would ask if they could move up the timeline since Blake has to move to Los Angeles. Kacey gave her a quizzical look.

"Are they just going to let you schedule the internship? That sounds like an adult thing."

"Why not, Mr. Fluffington has already passed most of the classes. He only has two more and we're almost done with those."

"I don't know, adults are weird sometimes."

Ashley knew Kacey was right, adults were weird sometimes. She had hoped that everything would go smoothly with the coordinator, but if she didn't let her move up the timeline, she would need a backup plan. Time was tight. Ashley couldn't let anything slow down Mr. Fluffington's progress.

————

The day of the meeting, Ashley rushed home from school and grabbed Mr. Fluffington. She planned to get there at 4:30pm so they could be in and out before Papa George got home from work. They hopped on the train and rode downtown to University Dental. When they got there, Ashley's eyes almost popped out of their sockets. The building radiated oral excellence. The lobby was sharp and immaculate, shimmering mini-exhibits about dental history and glorious oil portraits of dental school deans. This was a dream come true. They walked past the front desk and took the elevator up to the clinic. They arrived a few minutes early, so Ashley sat patiently with Mr. Fluffington in the waiting room. One of the receptionists gave her an odd look. She figured that they probably didn't see a lot of dogs in the office, but they would have to get used to it once Mr. Fluffington started his internship!

When the Internship Coordinator arrived, Ashley leapt up to shake her hand. "Hi, Ms. Collins, I'm Ashley."

"Excuse me?"

"Ashley Kippinger, we have a meeting—"

"About an internship placement?"

"Yes! For…"

"For Demitri Fluffington, he's right here." Ashley pointed at Mr. Fluffington, who was sitting quietly with a polite smile on his face and his tongue excitingly flopping about.

"Is this a prank or something?"

"No no no! Mr. Fluffington has completed the required courses for the internship placement and—"

"Listen, I'm sorry, there must have been a miscommunication. Are your parents here?" Mr. Fluffington could tell something was wrong, he walked over to Ashley's leg and started whimpering.

"What? No umm, he's still at work and…" Mr. Fluffington started to softly yap. "Mr. Fluffington, please, I've got this."

"We really can't have a dog in here, we need to move to the hallway then we can figure out what's going on." Mr. Fluffington's yaps turned to barks. "And can you please quiet your dog!"

"But I, but we–" Mr. Fluffington's barks grew louder, he started to pull on the leash in Ashley's hand. Her eyes started welling up, this was not supposed to happen.

"Please! Now! If you don't move the dog, then I will!"

"But–"

The coordinator grabbed at Mr. Fluffinton's leash. Without thinking, Ashley jumped back and dropped the handle. Mr. Fluffington took off. He sped through the waiting room, past the reception desk, and down the hallway. Behind him, the coordinator shouted, "Someone grab that dog!"

A rush of excitement shot through Mr. Fluffington. He had never seen dental technology like this before! Yes, he had studied the books and listened to the lectures, but to see all the tools and machines up close and in real life was incredible! He ran into one room and saw a bulky camera on a long rotating arm. That must be the x-ray machine! He sniffed around and felt the fine craftsmanship on the flexible joints. He scurried to the other side of the machine and saw the slick and intuitive design on the control panel. How he would love to see the images this machine could conjure.

Next, he slipped into an operatory, where a dental student was inspecting the teeth of a middle-aged man. Look at that dental chair, he thought, comfortable for the patient and providing maximum range of movement for the perfect inspection angle. Mr. FLuffington barked to let the student know what a good job he was doing, and the student jumped so high he knocked over his tray of tools onto the floor. Whoops! Mr. Fluffington barked again to let him know that he was sorry and didn't mean to scare him. A few of the tools landed by his paws so he nudged them over to the tray and then darted out of the room.

Back in the hallway, he saw quite the commotion. The coordinator and multiple other staff members were running in his direction. There must be something exciting this way! Mr. Fluffington didn't want to get in their way, so he decided to stay put and see where would lead him, what more magical dental wonders they had in store.

———

When Papa George arrived, a security officer met him out front. Ashley could see them exchanging words, mostly the guard talking and Papa George nodding along. Inside the lobby, the Internship Coordinator held Mr. Fluffington's leash with a clenched fist and kept his torso pinned in between her legs. Ashley sat on a bench next to them. This was a disaster. There was no way they were going to let Mr. Fluffington do his internship now, and the deadline had passed to apply to all the other internship sites. But she wasn't going to give up. If they couldn't find an internship placement for Mr. Fluffington, they would have to make do on their own.

Ashley was glad that Kacey sat down with her at recess. Without their backup plan, she would be lost. While Mr. Fluffington was exploring the dental clinic, Ashley was able to use the commotion as cover and snag some of their dental tools so they could set up a practice clinic of their own at home. She didn't take anything the clinic didn't have a million of, some mirrors and forceps, a few scalers and probes. She even got her hands on a small drill with foot pedals, perfect for Mr. Fluffington's paws. University Dental would have been great, but they didn't need their fancy machines or facilities. They could do all the internship assignments on their own, surely the dental school staff would applaud their ingenuity.

———

Ashley could see Papa George fuming as he drove them back home. When they arrived he cooly told her to put Mr. Fluffington in her room and then come back out to the kitchen. She did as she was told. He was sitting at the kitchen table when she returned, and before she could say anything, he bellowed, "Ashley what on earth were you thinking?!"

"Papa George, I–"

"Ashley, I don't want to hear it, I don't want to hear any of it. This dental school joke has gone on long enough."

"It's not a joke!"

"It is a joke! And it's not funny any more! People could have been hurt! Imagine if the dog ran into someone while they were operating on someone or tripped them while they were walking with the sharp tools."

"It was the woman's fault! She shouldn't have been yelling–"

"Ashley, this was too far. I never should have let it get to this point. I thought you were mature enough to have a pet, but I was wrong."

"I am mature!"

"I'm taking the dog away."

"WHAT?!"

"It's one thing to spend all your time with it, it's another to get so far into this fantasy that you're putting other people in danger."

"You can't!"

"This is not a discussion. Mr. Fluffington is going to go to a pet hotel for the time being, and I'll decide what to do with him next."

"Papa–"

"Go say your goodbye, I'm leaving with him in five minutes."

Ashley ran crying to her room. This couldn't be happening, Papa George couldn't take Mr. Fluffington away. They were so close to finishing the semester, they would have to start all over if he missed the final exam! She had no friends here, school was a drag…Mr. Fluffington was all she had and she was not going to let him go.

She grabbed Mr. Fluffington and they hid under her bed. She told him what was happening and Mr. Fluffington let out a whimper. She shushed him and they curled up together in silence, waiting for what was to come.

A few minutes later, she could hear Papa George's footsteps coming down the hall. He called out, "Ashley, this is it, say goodbye to the dog." Ashley closed her eyes as tight as she could, maybe if she couldn't see, then Papa George wouldn't find her. She heard the door open and Papa George's footsteps came closer and closer. He paused right near the bed. She held her breath and gripped Mr. Fluffington tight. She could feel the floorboards shift under Papa George's weight. Maybe he would change his mind, maybe if she could hide here long enough he would realize how much this would break her. Papa George's arm shot under the bed and grabbed her. Ashley started to scream and Mr. Fluffington howled, but none of it stopped Papa George from dragging her out from under the bed. Ashley held Mr. Fluffington as tight as she could, but Papa George slowly pried her arms apart and separated Mr. Fluffington from her grasp. He turned around and walked out of the room.

Ashley chased after, tears clouding her vision. She tried to yell but nothing would come out. It felt like she was choking on air. She lunged for Papa George, but his strides were too long and she tripped on her own legs, crumpling to the ground. She wiped her eyes and looked up towards the front door, Blake was standing there with a dog crate and Papa George was forcing Mr. Fluffington in. Ashley tried to yell but could only gasp, "Blake, don't!" Blake's eyes were glued to the floor, he wasn't even looking at Papa George, just holding the crate. Once Mr. Fluffington was in the crate, Papa George locked the door and whispered something into Blake's ear. Ashley tried to crawl to the door, anything she could to stop them, but she felt like she was suffocating and could barely even get up on her knees. Papa George kissed Blake on the cheek, then Blake turned and left with Mr. Fluffington. Papa George remained in the doorway. The room started to spin as Ashley watched the door close behind Blake. Everything turned black and she collapsed onto the floor.

— — —

For the next month, Ashley felt like she was in a trance. She sleptwalked through school, food tasted bland, the sun didn't shine as bright. Her life had lost meaning. Papa George tried to cheer her up, but she wanted no part of his family outings and ice cream sundaes. Her body tensed whenever he came near. He even offered to throw Ashley a big birthday party, anything she wanted and she could invite anyone from school, but she couldn't imagine celebrating at a time like this.

She tried to keep up with the dental school lessons for when Mr. Fluffington came back, but without him by her side, she lost all motivation. Instead of lesson planning and organizing at recess, she would just sit in the corner of the gym and stare off into space. Kacey would stop by to say hi, but Ashley had nothing to say to her. She could never understand.

One day, Kacey plopped down next to her and wouldn't stop yammering about Winona and how she had certified in massage therapy. She eventually wore her down, and Ashley spilled everything. The clinic visit, Papa George taking away Mr. Fluffington, the despair she was feeling. Even the birthday party. Kacey told her if the offer for a party was on the table, she might as well take advantage, she wished her dad would do that. She said that maybe if she was really well behaved and started having friends, Papa George would let her get Mr. Fluffington back. They could go to a musical or something and show Papa George how mature they were. Ashley's brain had felt submerged in darkness since Mr. Fluffington was taken away, but suddenly, a sliver of light emerged.

"Kacey, if we got to go to a musical, are there two more people you could invite?"

"Sure, I can ask Lizzy and Tess."

"Great."

"Why?"

"I have an idea, but I'll need your help."

— — —

Two weeks later, Ashley sat in a minivan with Papa George, Blake, Kacey, Lizzy, and Tess. They were on the road to see some silly boy band musical that Kacey was obsessed with. Ashley and Kacey had gone over the plan a dozen times, everything was ready to go. Lizzy and Tess had no clue what was going on, they just needed to be extras in her production. Once they got to their seats and the curtains rose, Ashley was so excited she could barely pay attention to the musical. The songs flew by and soon it was intermission. Showtime.

Ashley and Kacey met in the bathroom. Ashley took out the small block of cheese she had snuck in.

"You sure you'll be okay?" Ashley asked.

"Yeah yeah, I just throw up for a bit and then my stomach calms down, it's happened before."

Ashley hugged Kacey, "Thank you so much for doing this."

"Absolutely. If it were Winona locked away, I'd feel the same way."

They returned to their seats and right as the lights began to dim, Kacey took the cheese from her pocket and began to chew. She felt her mouth start to water and her stomach start to churn. Her tongue went numb and her gums tingled, but she forced the cheddar down. Five seconds later, an unholy gurgle emanated from her belly. She turned to Papa George.

"Excuse me, Ashley's Dad…I think I'm going to be sick."

"Can it wait?"

"No, I feel like I'm going to, uhh, I'm going to–"

Kacey began to wretch and Papa George's eyes bulged. He saw her face turn pale and her hand shot to her mouth. He swiftly grabbed Kacey by her armpits, lifted her right up out of her seat, and ran with her out to the theater lobby. They weren't going to have time to get to the restroom, so he scanned the lobby and saw a standing flower vase. Papa George swung Kacey over and held her above it as the cheese reversed its course and began flying from her mouth.

In the theater, Ashley watched as Blake frantically looked around for Papa George. She had made sure to sit at the other end of the row, and just as the doe-eyed boys danced back on stage, Ashley whispered to Lizzy, "Hey, if Blake asks, I had to run out and use the bathroom." Lizzy nodded and returned her eyes to the stage. She didn't give a shit. Lizzy had only talked to Ashley once or twice before tonight, she was just here for the show. The perfect accomplice.

Once she got into the lobby, Ashley crouched down and duck-walked out. Most of the lobby staff were helping Papa George and Kacey, who had been returned to the ground, but was still slumped over the flower pot, so no one noticed as Ashley exited the front door into the cold Boston evening.

When she got to the pet hotel, the attendant asked how she could help her, and Ashley said that she was there to pick up Mr. Fluffington. She told the woman that he was in long-term holding, but her mom had called earlier tonight to let them know she would be coming to get Mr. Fluffington for the weekend. The attendant clicked around her computer for a few seconds and said, "Is your Mom here with you? We usually don't release pets to people under eighteen." People always told Ashley that her braces made her look older, she never really cared one way or the other, but tonight it might play to her advantage. She stood up tall and responded, "My mom is out in the car waiting, her name is Blake Nylan, she should be on Mr. Fluffington's contact list. She dropped her off a month ago and she called earlier to say I would be coming to pick him up." The woman clicked around her computer some more then nodded in approval. She would be out with the dog right away.

As soon as Ashley got outside, she grabbed Mr. Fluffington out of the crate and hugged him with all her might. The crate bounced on the sidewalk and she kicked it into the street, they wouldn't be needing that anymore. She nuzzled Mr. Fluffington into her face and said, " I missed you so so so so much Mr. Fluffington." Then she held him at arm's length and looked deep into his eyes, "But I hope you're ready, because we have work to do."

Ashley and Mr. Fluffington scampered to the train and made it home with ease. If Kacey's districation lasted as long as she said it would, they would have plenty of time to set up and get started. When they got inside, Ashley bolted the doors, closed the security latches, and pushed the kitchen table right up to the front door – just to be safe. Mr. Fluffington pranced around the home while Ashley collected his dental tools, but as she was bringing them into the living room, she was interrupted by the sound of the front door unlocking and the latch catching the door. Shit. Papa George must have figured out she was gone earlier than she planned. Papa George stuck his mouth into the gap and yelled, "Ashley, let me in! ASHLEYYY!" They would have to start right away.

Ashley calmly positioned the recliner under the lamp and dumped their collection of dental tools onto the table. Mr. Fluffington joined her and took his place next to the tools. Ashley bent down to plug in the drill, then fit the dental headset onto Mr. Fluffington's head. He looked very cute in his dental gear, she couldn't wait to get some professional photos taken for his practice.

Papa George's incessant banging on the door would be a mild distraction, but nothing Mr. Fluffington couldn't handle. Ashley took her seat in the chair, draped a bib over her chest, and then placed the drill in Mr. Fluffington's waiting paws. She could see Papa George through the window, furiously trying to kick in the front door. Ashley hated that narrow entryway when they first moved in, but now she could see its merits. She made sure the tools were nice and neat one last time and pointed the lamp towards her face. Looking back at Mr. Fluffington, she asked, "This good?"

Mr. Fluffington arffed in approval and Ashley opened her mouth as wide as she could. Papa George stopped kicking and looked on in shock as Mr. Fluffington bounced his head, dropping his face shield into place. Then, Mr. Fluffington focused his attention on the cavity in Ashley's first bicuspid, pressed the on button with his back paw, and slowly lowered the drill into her mouth.

Tequilas and Mezcals

Write and Wrong Cocktail Lounge Specials

Tequila Mockingbird

2 oz blanco tequila

4 oz sweet tea

0.25 oz simple syrup

Garnish with a blackberry

Serve righteously

All the King's Mezcal

1 oz Espadín mezcal

1 oz Tobalá mezcal

1 oz Tobaziche mezcal

1 oz Tepeztate mezcal

1 oz Arroqueño mezcal

1 oz agave nectar

2 oz lime juice

9 oz ginger ale

Garnish with a lime wedge

Serve extremely carefully

Lime and Punishment
Muddle mint leaves in a cold glass
1 oz blanco tequila
1 oz joven tequila
1 oz reposado tequila
1 oz añejo tequila
1 lime's worth of juice
1 oz simple syrup
4 oz soda
Garnish with a lime ring
Serve with anguish

The House on Mezcal Street
2 oz mezcal
2 oz mango puree
4 oz soda
A squeeze of lime
Rim the glass with Tajín,
Garnish with a mango wedge
Serve bildungsromanly

2

Civics

The truth is, selling lessons is not the business it used to be. My family has sold lessons to generations, as far back as the family tree goes. Schools need their teachers, and teachers need their lessons, and we are always there to provide. My family tells of ancestors who scribbled notes on John Dewey's chalkboard and encouraged young Maria Montessori to explore her true passions. Uncle Alexandros even tells of how it was our many-many-great-great-grandfather who told Socrates to stop lecturing so damn much and let the kids speak!

So, ladies and gentlemen of the jury, you may be asking yourselves, why is this seller of lessons on trial today? Is he a hardened criminal? A mastermind of misdeed and felony? Most certainly not! What happened was all one big misunderstanding, and after my testimony today, you will see that I am not guilty of any crimes. In fact, a crime was committed against *me*! My livelihood was stolen, and I was simply trying to retrieve what is rightfully mine.

Like I made mention, business has waned. Sure, some of us still do well…Cousin Omar is the personal advisor in charge of lessons to the Hashemite King of Jordan, imagine that! And Aunt Maria sells lessons to the entire municipality of São Paulo, millions of students receive her lessons every day. Me, I have just my humble shop on Marcellin Street. My grandmother is always telling me, Korman, why don't you sell more lessons like your cousins? Why don't you try and sell to the city? I tell her, Grandma, it's not that simple. I try, I try, but it's not easy. I so badly wish to be able to show up to family holidays and brag to Cousin Omar and Aunt Maria for once, to have Grandma tell everyone about how she saw my face on the news. Everyone knows my lessons are top-notch, place and time is the only reason I am still stuck on Marcellin Street.

Sadly, my place and time have looked even less fortuitous recently. When MegaLesson opened their big store downtown, I could not compete with their volume and all the teachers began to flock there. I went in once to see the competition, and I could not believe that any reputable teacher would shop there. The layout was bare and harsh, the lessons were wrapped in plastic so you could not inspect them before purchase, and the staff did not know the first thing about what they were selling! Their product is low-quality and vapid, a shell of a true lesson. And don't even let me start on the web sites.

My current customers are a small but loyal group. They return to my shop because I sell the best, hand-crafted, artisanal lessons in the city. Sometimes the teachers and I will take the bland lessons their schools give them and punch them up, but I prefer we start from scratch and craft something beautiful together. Unique, like a snowflake on a fingerprint. It can be a wonderful partnership – teachers don't have time to ponder over each lesson like I do, they spend their time teaching! Young teachers, old teachers, new teachers, experienced teachers; I work with all of them, and together we make the best lessons so the youth can learn and grow. They are custom-made for each classroom and are guaranteed to be effective. That's a Korman promise.

When MegaLesson first started stealing my customers, I tried to make up for the lost business by photocopying my best lessons and selling them on the street. But after a week it began to feel like a betrayal of my values. I would rather go out of business one-thousand times than compromise on the quality of my lessons. Sure, profits are down, but I will find a way to keep my store afloat. I always do.

By now you may be thinking, so Korman, what was stolen from you? Did someone break into your shop and pilfer your lessons? No, no, it was nothing like that. As you will see, the story of theft is a tangled web indeed.

— — —

It began last fall when a flustered young woman entered my shop. I watched as she started rummaging through my pre-made lessons, aimlessly drifting from shelf to shelf. I used to see her type more often; wide-eyed, bushy-tailed, full of hope and fear. Now it is a rarity, new teachers are given so many students and so little time to plan that they usually just take what lessons the school gives them. I made sure to treat her with care, like a baby bird that had fallen out of the nest. I sang out to her, excuse me my friend! How may I help you today?

She looked over and mumbled something about needing new lessons. I told her she was in the exact right place and asked what she taught. She walked over to my counter and before saying a word, her eyes wandered to my computer. She reached out and touched the three lines scratched into the back of my computer's screen. I asked if she was in the market for an old, decaying laptop. She asked if I got it for a good price. I said, of course, the best price, I would not pay a cent more. She asked if I bought it from Edwin Lee.

Who was she, I thought, the police? Sure, Mr. Edwin and I used to joke about his laptops falling off the back of a truck, and his prices were quite low, but I bought this laptop years ago and hadn't spoken to Mr. Edwin since then. Almost all the small shops on this side of the city got our computers from Mr. Edwin – we couldn't afford them from anyone else! I did not enjoy the fact that he may have gotten them from a disreputable source, it made me queasy for many weeks in fact, but I needed a computer and could not afford one from the store. What did she want to do, interrogate me? Bring me down to the station and shine a lamp in my eyes and slam her hand on the table and say, dammit Korman, tell me the truth?

But no. She told me Edwin Lee was her father, and she used to help him sell his laptops around the city when she was young. She said he would always tell her that it was important to provide for the people who are doing the most good for the community. How true! I asked how he was doing, and she told me he was well, but wasn't in sales anymore. The man he got his goods from had a complicated situation, so he mostly works in real estate now, and is doing quite well for himself. I was pleased to hear this, I always knew Edwin Lee to be a fair and decent man. I turned to my new friend and said, so, the daughter of Edwin Lee, what is your name? Rosa, she told me. I am Korman, I said, and how may I help you today, Ms. Rosa?

She had just started teaching at the school down the street from my shop, Warren School Elementary, and she was already feeling behind the mule. I told her I was surprised she didn't just go to MegaLesson like all of the other teachers, and she said she actually was just there an hour ago, but she found their lessons dull and uninspiring. I could tell Rosa was sharp from the beginning. Pull up a chair, I told her, tell me about your classroom.

Rosa sat down and told me of how she had signed up for a training program for new teachers where she would be a student teacher for a year at Warren School, but in the first week, one of the 3rd grade teachers left and they told her she would be like a substitute teacher until they could find a replacement. It was becoming clear that there was no replacement coming, so she would be no student of teachers this year but a teacher of students. She told me how most of the students were behind on reading and math, and that she would spend hours trying to come up with lessons that would engage them and help them learn, but every day something would go wrong. One day it was a fire drill, another day Isaiah and Declan got into a fight, and just yesterday Kaylani decided to show the class how she knew the entire dance to that summer's most popular song, and when Rosa tried to get her to settle down the class booed her into submission.

I told Rosa, my dear, you have quite a meal on your plate! Let us make you a lesson that will knock the socks off your classroom, free of charge. We chose a theme that was specific yet universal, we selected activities that involved movement and thought and calculation and deduction, we assigned specific roles to specific students based on their wants and needs, hopes and dreams. This lesson truly was a thing of beauty; complex yet accessible, familiar yet brand new. The Rhapsody in Blue of classroom activities! Now that I think about it, I bet the ladies and gentlemen of the jury would value seeing this lesson. Your honor, may I motion to put this lesson plan into the record of evidence? No, I may not? Okay, okay, but I assure you it was truly spectacular. Anyway, when we finished and looked at the clock, it was already half past nine! How time flies when magic is being made. Rosa packed up her things, pushing aside the pigsty of papers in her bag so she could neatly place the lesson inside, and told me she would come visit tomorrow to let me know how the lesson went.

The next evening Rosa burst into my shop with a smile brighter than two-hundred and nineteen suns. Korman, she said, what a success the lesson was! She told me about how the students were laughing and learning the whole day. How they were engaged and active, helping each other to read and write. How they told her how much fun school was today and how they couldn't wait for tomorrow. She said she needed another lesson and quickly! I knew she would, so I had already prepared enough for the rest of the week. I said, Ms. Rosa, take these and then come back every week and we will make more lessons. Then your class will be this good every day. Rosa asked how she could repay me, and I told her that starting next week, market rate will do! We laughed and laughed and laughed and laughed and she took the lessons and held them close to her heart and floated out of my shop. I had not been that happy in quite a while, perhaps my shop was not to be doomed, I thought.

— — —

After that, Rosa returned every week. Each time we would start by sitting and discussing her class – what parts of the lessons worked and what parts did not – and each week they would get better and better. The other teachers began to take notice and started asking her questions about her lessons. I would tell her that she should not be shy about telling the other jealous teachers where she got her lessons from! She would say, yes Korman, I will tell them, I will tell them. And wouldn't you know it, soon a trickle of teachers turned into a roaring river. Business was booming! Some would come and just pick a lesson off the shelf, others would ask for lesson repairs, a few would even sit with me to craft lessons together. But no one spent as much time with me as Rosa.

Fall turned to winter, winter turned to spring, and everything was right as rain, until one Friday in April when Rosa arrived at my shop with a cloud of sadness above her. I said, Ms. Rosa, what is the problem? Who has taken your umbrella and dumped water on your head? On this day she did not even crack a smile at my witticism, this was very unlike her. Instead, she sat down and said, Korman, I have the most unimaginable news. The city was to close down Warren School.

I asked her, how could this be? She had the best lessons in all of the city and many of the other teachers had slightly-less-good-but-still-excellent lessons as well. The children were thriving! She agreed that they were, but told me that their test scores came back and they did not have a good year. The tests! I said, who cares about the tests?! My lessons help the kids to learn about life, about deep thought and imagination, teamwork and trust, not how to fill in bubbles on a sheet of paper. Rosa shook her head, the city cares about tests. She said the school also had many open desks and so the city had cut their budget, they had to let go of the art teacher and the music teacher and the man who walks around with the walkie-talkie muttering about the kids needing therapy. All of the teachers were told that next week, the School Committee would vote to close the school after this year ended and the students would be moved to different schools.

I asked, Ms. Rosa, what will we do? What other schools will you apply to teach at? She said she could not even think of a question like that at a time like this. She was so pained to think about the students she would no longer see and the families that would scatter throughout the city. She got up and paced around my store, listing all the injustices being done to them. I couldn't have agreed with her more, but I was trying to help her feel better, so I told her I was sure she would land on her feet. This must have struck a deep chord within her because she turned to me and shouted, Korman, it is not about me! The children, the school, the community, think about what they are doing to us! We can stop this, she declared, we must stop this!

Now, most of my lessons are for schools, yes, but I know a little bit about the world outside the classroom as well. I asked Rosa if she had a plan and she slumped down in her chair. Not yet Korman, she said, do you have any lessons for me about keeping a school open? I said, Ms. Rosa, I have one lesson and I will give it to you four times: organize, organize, organize, organize. Rosa nodded along, she said, yes Korman, we must organize the community. We must plan for action! First, we will need a place to gather the group, she said. As it just so happens, I have a cousin who owns a nice hall that he rents out for weddings, so I prayed that love was not in the air that week, because I told Rosa I would get us a space if she could get the people. The meeting would happen that Monday.

She returned the next day with electricity coursing through her veins and told me that not only were parents and students going to come in droves, but most of the teachers agreed to come and lend their support as well! We knew we needed to make a big splash, so we spent all night working on our plan for the meeting. The speech to the parents and teachers would be the easy part, it was the action to convince the School Committee to not close Warren School that was the challenge. Rosa asked if I had any lessons on civil disobedience, and I told her, as a matter of fact, I did have a few in my back pocket. How disobedient did she want to be? She said, Korman, I want to hear the craziest shit you have. Ha! I had just the lesson.

We had agreed that Rosa would give the opening speech and then I would step in and introduce our grand plan. We arrived at my cousin's venue early, and I helped set up the chairs and the refreshments while Rosa stood at the door and greeted our defenders of Warren School. Once everyone was seated and had their paper cups of lemonade and finger sandwiches, we mounted the stage and began the program. I was so excited to share in leadership of this event, if only Grandma could see me tonight!

Everything started out according to plan. Rosa welcomed everyone to the meeting and even gave me an unexpected salute in the beginning of her speech. She said I was the finest provider of lessons in the whole city and many of the teachers thought I was as much a part of the school as they were. How kind of her! Then she built and built and built, telling everyone of the injustice of the closing of our school and how only we the people, organized for action, could stop it. The crowd was on their feet! She reached her grand conclusion, and it was my turn to tell everyone about our plan, but instead of stopping, she continued to speak and told them the plan herself. Now, I am a good sport, so I did not say anything at the time. I always put the good of the community ahead of my own desires. But, to be truthful, I was quite upset. It was my plan after all, and I was supposed to be the one to share it with the group. She had stepped on my feet! But the show must go on, and after Rosa told everyone about the plan for the fart-in at the School Committee meeting, the crowd roared in approval. I put all my chagrin aside and could not help but smile. After all, I had been saving this lesson for years and could not wait to see it in action.

Rosa and I had plans to meet the next night at my shop to go over her weekly lessons, but at our arranged time, Rosa was nowhere to be found. When I called her, she apologized and said she was too busy organizing for the meeting. She had just used the lessons the school gave her this week. Can you imagine? Those children must have been bored out of their minds with the slop the school serves after months of my homemade lessons. Nevertheless, we had a plan.

She had been meeting with the parents and teachers to practice for the meeting, and she assured me we were ready.

— — —

On Wednesday, the School Committee convened. The Warren School team met outside the meeting room for one last huddle, and after Rosa confirmed that our team had eaten enough baked beans and cheesy burritos to stress test a pressure cooker, we walked together to take our seats. The meeting room was short and wide, chairs were set in a semicircle pointed at the front where the School Committee members sat behind their raised desks. We spread out, sitting two-by-two and three-by-three around the whole perimeter for maximum coverage. Rosa would give the signal when it was her turn to speak during public comment. The School Committee was scheduled to vote on the fate of Warren School right after, so we needed to be loud and proud if we were to have a chance at success.

Once the meeting started, we sat politely and clenched tightly as other community members spoke to the School Committee. After thirty minutes, it was finally Rosa's turn. This was not the same Rosa who had stumbled into my shop a few short months ago. This Rosa was as proud as a lion, and she spoke with such passion and courage about the Warren School community and the importance of the school to the families that send their children there. She spoke about how much of what the children were learning could not be measured by a test, and how much they all grew every day. We all cheered in support and the chairman of the School Committee became so perturbed that two times he asked for quiet. But Rosa was cool as a kumquat, and after the cheering calmed, she looked straight at him and said, Mr. Chairman, excuse my French, but we think the decision to close Warren Elementary School is a big pile of bullshit!

The Chairman banged his gavel and barked, Ms. Lee! There is no need for–, but before he could finish, he was interrupted by a sound from the audience. It was a deep, rumbling squall of hot air that turned every head, and before the Chairman could continue, more gas began to emerge. Soon a whole chorus of flatulence had sprang forth from the Warren School community! Farts were coming strong from the left and strong from the right, creating a stereoscopic ass-ripping ruckus. The children cut their cheese at a high pitch, staccato bursts of broken wind that added a lovely harmony to the lower-toned releases from the adults. One of the more sophisticated parents was even able to toot out the first few notes of "Ode to Joy." A proctological Pavarotti!

The School Committee members were confused and disgusted, but their ordeal had only just begun. While they were engrossed by the noise, we all donned our paper face masks, and our silent-but-deadly team got to work. They took out their hand fans, passed their gas, and began furiously fanning towards the School Committee at the front of the room. The noxious odor built and built, and people began to cough and retch, and just as the chorus of flatulence was reaching a crescendo, one of the fathers let rip a wet, monstrous fart that sounded like a gallon of thick soup hitting cement after being dumped from a second-story window. These were not the sounds of a healthy man. And indeed he was not, as after his grand finale, he whispered, uh-oh, and a dripping began from his pant leg. This was not in the plan, but I must admit, it was a nice touch.

The Chairman could not find his gavel in the chaos and resorted to slamming his hand on the desk, shouting, Order! Order! But there could be no order as the crowd rushed towards the doors to escape the fumes. School Committee members jumped from their chairs and raced alongside the crowd, climbing over each other to get to the aisles and shoving their way to the exits, desperate for fresh air. Just as we planned, our team sat patiently until everyone else had exited, then we calmly rose and walked to the lobby. Bringing up the rear was our soup-butted friend, who waddled out of the room, leaving a trail of hot tar in his wake.

The Chairman was forced to call the meeting into recess and when the custodial staff arrived to assess the situation, they told him the room was now a biohazard zone and it would have to be closed off for hours, if not days, to fully clean. The School Committee was forced to reschedule all votes to the meeting the following week. We had done it! Warren School had lived to see another day, and after we all changed into the extra pairs of pants we'd brought along, our team claimed victory outside of the building where the local TV news was waiting. A little bird had let them know they would want to be there, and they were all eager to talk to the star of the show. They wanted Rosa.

All the TV news stations fought to interview her, and by the time they left, she had told each and every one of them the whole story of Warren School and our fight to stay open. All across the city, people watched Rosa give an impassioned defense of Warren School, and the next morning her picture was on the front page of every newspaper! People began to call and email Rosa, asking how they could help keep Warren School open. We told them to send their calls and emails to the School Committee, because it is in their hands now. The TV news wanted Rosa back every night to give them updates, the city fell in love with her! Some local politicians even started to join our cause; a State Senator wanted to speak on our behalf at the next School Committee meeting and two City Counselors told us that they would speak to Mayor O'Malley to see what he could do. Perhaps they were just riding our wave, but if it helps to keep Warren School open, I say ride away!

Even as she was doing the TV news and the newspaper interviews, Rosa still came by my shop every night so we could plan our next move. I would say, Ms. Rosa, you have become quite a star! I hope you do not forget little old me. And she would say, of course I won't Korman, how could I forget you? We planned the community meetings throughout the week and held a big rally on the City Commons during the weekend. There must have been five hundred people in attendance! We could not believe how many people came to support us. We told them all to call the School Committee and their State Senators and City Counselors and everyone down to the Dog Catchers to tell them to vote no' to closing Warren School. They cheered with such gusto I thought I would cry.

The night before the next School Committee meeting, Rosa and I sat at my shop and discussed our plan. She would lead our group to sit in the audience, but this time we would not interrupt. The vote would be held, and it would be up to the School Committee to decide the fate of Warren School. Rosa had become the talk of the town, and I knew her heart was pure, but that much attention can knock a person off-balance. When I expressed my concern, she just rolled her eyes and said, Korman, do not worry about me, I will not lose focus of the goal. I said, Ms. Rosa, of course you will not, but allow me to tell you a story that I think will illustrate my point. She laughed and said, okay, I have time for one lesson, then I must go.

I told her of my many-many-great-great Grandmother who lived on a small island in the Pacific Ocean. Her family had lived there happily for many generations, but one year the fish did not visit their sea and the rain did not fall and after many months they had little left to eat, so they decided to travel by boat to a neighboring island. All the families built small canoes and set off into the sea, but no matter how hard they paddled, the tides always moved them back. They thought perhaps the ocean was not happy, and they would try again the next day. In the morning, they all set off again, but the same thing happened. They paddled all day against the ocean, but could not advance, and were all washed back to shore. By the third day, they were distraught. They had almost nothing left, and if they could not leave the island soon, they would surely perish. They set off a third time and that morning they still made no progress. By midday, my many-many-great-great Grandmother's family grew tired and floated next to another family's boat to rest. The children teased each other and grabbed each other's boats, holding them together so they could hop from one to the other and back. While they were doing this, she noticed that they were more stable, not floating backwards quite as quickly. She called out to the other boats, and they paddled over. The children were instructed to hold on to the boat next to them, and when the adults paddled forward, they were able to push against the tide and travel to the next island. Apart we move backwards, my many-many-great-great Grandmother discovered, only together will we move forward.

— — —

The next night, we all met outside the Central Office, and with just a short speech, Rosa lit a fire under the behinds of our supporters. We marched up to the School Committee meeting and filled the room to capacity. There were even people waiting outside in the hallway, listening to the voices through the wall and cheering and jeering along with the people inside. When it came time to vote, the School Committee members looked nervous. They had been so arrogant last week, but we had rattled them. The public support we had received that week was undeniable. When it came time to vote, you should have seen the looks on their faces as they all voted no to closing Warren School! The crowd erupted in celebration, we danced and hugged and cheered in joy. The Chairman banged his gavel to finalize the vote, and the Warren School families lifted Rosa onto their shoulders and carried her out of the room in victory. It was exhilarating! In fact, I have some pictures here that I clipped from the newspaper. Your honor, may I motion to show these pictures to the jury? I think they would like to see them. No? One more motion and my testimony will be over? Well, motion withdrawn then, we cannot let that happen. We have much more to discuss.

Time seemed to fly by after our victory. I had many end-of-year lessons to prepare for all the teachers, and Rosa was so busy teaching and keeping the community group organized that she hadn't come into my shop for many weeks. I did not see her until the last week of the school year when she walked into my store with a very serious look on her face. I said, Ms. Rosa, my dear! It is great to see you, to what do I owe this honor? She said, Korman, sit down. I have some news to share. I promptly took my seat and told her, please! She took a deep breath and told me about how after the School Committee vote, she had been approached by a City Counselor who told her he was a big fan and was very impressed with her work. He told her there was a group of people who wanted to meet with her, a collection of many prominent politicians and professionals from the area. City elections were coming up in the fall and they wanted her to run for mayor against the incumbent, Mayor O'Malley.

His reputation may precede him, but it's true that Mayor O'Malley is a shark. He was in his second term as mayor and thought to be a shoo-in for a third. Born into a political family, he was a machine man from the day he was old enough to vandalize his opponents' campaign signs. A master of saying the right thing and doing nothing, he had recently blocked a new affordable housing development because it would bring too much traffic to the park where he takes his morning walks. People did not love him, but he was more entrenched than a donkey in quicksand, and due to his tendency to crush any and all opposition, no one with anything to lose wanted to run against him.

I asked, Ms. Rosa, what will you do? She looked at me and said, Korman, I'm going to run, and I'm going to win. How exciting it was! She thanked me for all I had done for her so far and told me she would need my help if she wanted to win. I agreed wholeheartedly! She told me she would be very busy and would not be able to stop by as often, but she was announcing her candidacy next week and she wanted me to be there. Of course I would be there, I was so excited and proud of her. Think of it, nine months ago she was a teacher without a clue, and now, under my tutelage, she might be mayor of our great city! Before she left, I asked her one thing, I said, Ms. Rosa, promise me you will do this the right way. These elections can get very dirty and I would hate to see you throw away what makes the people of the city love you. Things like this cannot be done by squeezing the fruit of all its juice. She said, of course Korman, I know, I know. And just know this. When I am mayor, there will be a special place for you as the chief lesson giver of the city. It will be a special post! To me, that sounded like a beautiful plan. Imagine me, Korman, Chief Lesson

Giver of the city. Imagine what the look on Cousin Omar's face would be!

When the big day came, I wore my best suit and got to the announcement early so I could sit in the front row. I tried to get a pass to sit backstage, but in the days before the announcement, Rosa was not picking up her phone. I figured she must have been busy, and she knew her old friend would still show up. So I arrived and I sat and when she walked onstage, the crowd exploded in cheers.

Rosa introduced herself, told everyone about her family and how they struggled when she was young. She talked of her plans for building more housing, improving public safety, and the cultural rebirth of our great city. She talked about her year as a teacher and how she learned more from the kids than they learned from her. I thought this would have been a nice place to give compliments to her old friend Korman, but nevertheless, it was an entrancing start. Then she slowed down and told us she wanted to share a story her grandmother had told her many years ago. I got so excited! I thought Rosa must have been inspired by the stories of my ancestors and decided to share the lessons from her own family history. But then she began to tell the story, it was about a village on a small island in the Pacific Ocean. I could not believe what I was hearing…I thought perhaps I had wax in my ears and it changed her words, but when I heard her tell about a bad harvest and the attempts to sail to another island, I knew it could be no mistake. My stomach dropped and the room began to spin. By the time I regained my balance she was telling everyone that apart we were destined to move backwards and only together can we move forward. I had been robbed! Yes, I had shared with her my story, but for her to claim it as her own without even a citation or reference, it is criminal! Then she waved her arms and behind her the curtain dropped from the massive campaign sign. It read, "Rosa Lee for Mayor - Forward Together." I felt like I was to throw up.

I laid awake that night and thought to myself that Rosa would have never done this to me by herself. It must have been that team of slimy politicians who put her up to it. She probably told them my story and they loved it so much that they insisted she claim it as her own. She probably pushed back, but they told her they would not give her the funds she needed if she did not use the story as her finale. By daylight, I decided I would have to talk to Rosa and get to the bottom of this.

The next morning, her campaign office was already bustling by the time I arrived. There were young adults stuffing envelopes, medium adults sending emails, and older adults sitting at large tables talking in hushed tones. I knocked on the door and one of the young adults cracked it open. I need to see Rosa, I told him. I'm sorry, she's in a meeting right now, he said. I told him to tell her Korman is here, and she will want to see me. But the young man shut the door on me! So I knocked again and again and again until one of the older men opened the door and told me to come with him. This man wore a suit and had prestigious hair, but I could tell he was a complete and total brute. As he walked me down a hallway he shouted at the mess of desks and a young man came running with a lighter. Without breaking a stride he took out a log of a cigar, stuck it between his teeth, lit it up, then tossed the lighter back at the chest of the young man. Not ten paces later we arrived at the end of the hallway and he motioned for me to sit down at a chair outside of the office. When I sat, he asked if there was anything he could get me, and I said, yes in fact there is! One of you forced Rosa to steal my story and you can get me the person who made her do this and have them tell me why they would start her campaign on such a lie! He asked me to calm down, and I said I would do no such thing! They were turning Rosa into something she was not, and I would not stand for it.

Rosa opened her office door and said, Korman! It is too early to be so worked up. Please, come in. She shooed the others away and led me into her office, telling me to please sit. I said, I will stand thank you very much! What have you done Ms. Rosa? Why did you let them make you steal my story? How do you hope to be mayor when you rest your campaign on a foundation of mistruth? She said Korman, please calm down, you do not understand this business. Aha! I said I understand it all too well. Korman, she said, I am not a teacher anymore, I don't need your lessons. Aha! I said, you need them more now than ever. Korman, she said, you have done very much for me, but I am trying to be mayor. I know you do not like what I did, but I would still love for you to be part of my team. I asked her how I could be a part of her team when she would do such a thing, and she said, you know how bad O'Malley has been to our community. We have a real chance to win here and make this city better for people like you and me, but O'Malley fights dirty and we have to be willing to roll around in the mud if we want to wrestle the pig. With that, she told me she was very busy and that I should call her if I needed anything else.

I left her office in a daze. Once I got back to my shop, I tried to focus on my work, but summertime is slow and the campaign was everywhere. On the TV, on the buses, even on the web videos my nephew would show me! It was a tough time for me, but I thought to myself, Korman, you have many lessons left and Rosa can never take from you what makes every day new. No one can do what I do, I am no common Korman. But the lesson block continued to grow day by day, until a week later when one night, there was a knock at my shop's door.

It was long past business hours, and I was not expecting any visitors, so I approached the door with caution. When I peeked outside, who did I see but Rosa Lee for Mayor. I thought my blood would boil to see her, but instead I felt quite gleeful. Some part of me must still have believed in the Rosa that I knew from before. Still, I decided to play it cool. I didn't want her to think I was some carpet that she could keep stepping on over and over again. I opened the door and said, Ms. Rosa, what a surprise. How may I help you tonight? She didn't say a word, and when she looked up at me I could see a deep sorrow across her face. I invited her inside and as soon as we sat down, tears started to well in her eyes. I said, Ms. Rosa, what is wrong? Korman, she said, what have I gotten myself into? She told me about how the campaign was consuming her whole life; she thought she would be able to make a change in the city, but instead she was spending most of her days asking rich people for donations and meeting with large groups of stuffy men. She barely even got to see any of our friends from Warren School, they were meeting without her and making new plans. She said that if she lost the election, she would be left with nothing.

But Ms. Rosa, I said, even if you lose you will still have Warren School! She shook her head. She had been so busy with the election that she had missed the deadline to apply for her full-time teaching position and Warren School had hired another teacher in her place. We talked for hours more. Yes, she was very popular and still had a chance to win, but O'Malley was as vindictive as they said. He had threatened to blacklist her campaign staff from future city jobs, and they started leaving one-by-one. She was starting to think they didn't even care about her vision in the first place, they just wanted someone to run against O'Malley so they could weaken him for the next election or the next-next election, and none of them wanted to be the focus of his ire. But even if they all abandoned her, she still believed, and she told me she would fight a polar bear in a snowstorm if it meant providing for our city.

It was almost sunrise by the time Rosa looked at the clock. She told me she had an event to be at in a few hours and perhaps should get some sleep. I nodded and said, Ms. Rosa, I'm glad you stopped by. I walked her to the door and before she left she said, Korman, I know my campaign has not been kind to you. I hope you can forgive me someday. Ms. Rosa, I said, how could I not?

— — —

Two weeks before the election, the race had narrowed, but Rosa was still behind in the polls. Anyone in the city could tell you that she needed an extra boost, so when she called a big press conference in front of Warren School, people flocked to the event to see what she would say. I had not seen her since she came to my shop that night, but we had been sending friendly emails back and forth, so I was surprised that she did not invite me personally. Either way, I am not one to take offense at petty grievances, so I walked over and got a spot nice and close to the stage. She started with her normal platitudes and slogans. Forward Together had been a big hit and when she said it in her speech, the crowd chanted along. From there, she said that to be mayor you needed more than big ideas and a sharp tongue, you needed to build a strong team to move the city forward. She had two announcements about this growing team. The first was that she had spoken with the company that worked on the affordable housing development the mayor blocked, and if elected mayor, they would be ready to resume construction on her first day in office. Sounded good to me! I was cheering along with the crowd, and Rosa looked over at our direction, so I gave her a big wave and thumbs-up in support. I thought it was odd that she did not wave back or smile, in fact, her eyes bulged out and she stammered her next few words, but at the time I just thought she was nervous by the size of the crowd.

Then she continued…the second announcement was that her campaign had been in conversation with MegaLesson, and that if she was elected mayor, they would partner to provide high quality, personalized lessons for every teacher in the city at a very reasonable price. She said it would revolutionize the education our schools would provide and make our city a leader in the nation. She said she even showed them the lessons she had been using this past school year and they were very excited to use those lessons as a template for the whole city. The next thing I remember was lying on my back and seeing the sky. A woman knelt next to me and asked if I was okay. I most certainly was not.

I walked back to my shop in despair. My head was held so low that I almost didn't see the man standing right next to my door. He asked if I was Korman. I said, who is asking? He said, I heard you are the victim of a theft by Rosa Lee for Mayor. He said he could help make things right. I invited him inside.

We sat down in my shop and I asked how he found me. He said he worked with the O'Malley for Mayor campaign and there might be a way we could help each other out. I asked him what his name was, and he said, perhaps it would be best if he does not share that with me. I was quite unnerved, but I must admit, my interest was piqued. He said that Mayor O'Malley wanted to meet with me and make a proposal that he thinks I would be interested in. He slid a card across the table and said I should show up at this address tomorrow at 8 o'clock in the AM. With that he got up and left, did not even have the courtesy to say goodbye. I looked at the card for many minutes, deeply considering what I should do. I did not want to get dragged any deeper into this business of campaigns…but he was the mayor after all. I figured, what harm could come from a short parley?

The next morning, I arrived at Avi's Delicatessen and was whisked to the back room. There sat Mayor O'Malley gobbling down a plate of corned beef hash. Next to him was one of his staff members, an intense man with eyes that peered deep into my soul. O'Malley looked up from his hash and yelped, Korman! Great to see, please sit down. Would you like anything to eat? I demurred. It was odd being this close to the man; I had seen him on the TV so many times. On the news, at ribbon-cuttings, at baseball games – but never this close. I had a funny feeling, but I must admit, it made me feel quite good that he knew my name. I was excited to call Grandma and tell her! Once I sat down, O'Malley put his fork on the table and said, Korman, I think there is a way we might be able to help each other out.

He told me that his campaign was going well, but Rosa was making it a closer race than they expected, and they wanted to give themselves some more insurance space in the polls. She had been getting nothing but good press from the start of her campaign; savior of Warren School, queen of the community, all of that fluff the news was serving. He said that he knew she had a tendency to take things that weren't hers, ran in the family, didn't it? I was taken aback. Did he know about Mr. Edwin? I thought it wise to stay quiet and just nod along. He told me that they needed to get some stories about that side of Rosa in the press, give the public a more complete picture of her character, and he thought I was just the person to help him do it.

Mayor O'Malley knew I was a friend to Rosa, even after what she had done to me. I was about to relay this to him when he held out his hand to stop me from even starting and said, Korman, I know you're thinking, why would I help him to betray my friend? He told me that if Rosa won, her deal with MegaLesson would almost certainly put me out of business. If all the teachers were getting lessons for free, why would they spend their money at my store? He was right, the future of my store was not bright if the MegaLesson deal was signed. So, he told me, here is what I will do for you. After Rosa's announcement, my team got in contact with LessonMax to get our own deal ready to go. He asked if I knew LessonMax and I said, of course, how could I not? They did not have any stores in our city yet, but rumors were that they were expanding from the West Coast and hoping to take a chunk out of MegaLesson's sales. O'Malley needed someone local to lead the lesson creation process for our city and if I helped them out, he would put me in charge of lessons for the deal. I would be well compensated for my work.

I was torn, I did not want to hurt my friend Rosa, but she had done nothing but take take take take from me recently, and this would give me a chance to bring lessons to the whole city. High-quality lessons. My lessons. I asked if I could have some time to think, but Mayor O'Malley shook his head. He said, unfortunately, we need an answer from you right now. If you do not want to do it, we will not be offended, but they need to move forward. If I did not want to lead the lessons and take my cut of the deal, they would find someone else to do it. What choice did I have?

They set up a meeting with a reporter for the next day. She had been told my story and was to interview me about Rosa's thefts. I arrived at Avi's Delicatessen at the agreed upon hour, but the reporter was nowhere to be found. I sat for a whole hour, twiddling my thumbs and snacking on dill pickles, but she never arrived. Instead, the intense man who was sitting next to O'Malley the day before barged in the front door and told me to follow him into the back room. I asked what had happened and he told me that the reporter had canceled on them.

Rosa's campaign was having an event that she decided to cover, and she withdrew just a few minutes ago. I asked what this meant for our deal, and he said, yes, very good. We still want to work with you, but now that the news story won't work, we have a different job for you. He reached into his pocket and pulled out a small plastic disc the size of a watch face. Korman, he said, take this and put it in Rosa's campaign office. You are a friend to her so you should have no problem getting in. Make up some excuse and call her for a meeting, it should be no problem.

What is this? I asked. He looked at me with growing agitation and said, don't be dense Korman, just get it done. I asked if there was another way for me to fulfill my end of the deal and he said there was not. He said if I did not do this then they would completely cut me out of the deal with LessonMax. The city would see sub-par lessons and I would be out in the cold.

— — —

That night, I put on my most discreet outfit and walked to Rosa's campaign office. If she was there with not too many other people, maybe I could find my way inside and plant the bug with minimal fuss. Quick in and out. Or maybe I would tell her about what Mayor O'Malley has asked me to do, and she would be so grateful that she would put me in charge of lessons again. I did not know what I would do, but when I arrived, the office was dark and empty. Not a single soul in sight. I grabbed the door handle and put my face to the window to look inside, I saw stacks of banners and posters piled high to the ceiling. Not only were they the Forward Together posters, but they had new ones. Big ones with the MegaLesson logo next to the Rosa for Mayor logo, and small ones with an image of linked boats floating in the ocean. Seeing those colorful illustrations of my betrayal must have unfastened something inside me, as I looked from stack to stack, my hands began to shake and I gripped the door handle harder and my body shook so vigorously that I heard a crack and suddenly the door popped open.

Now, I wouldn't usually enter a building without permission, but I was so angered by the garish display of what had been stolen from me that I was pulled by a magnetic force over to the pile of signs. I started loading my arms with as many as I could carry. After all, they were taken from me in the first place, I was in the right to take them back. I walked with them to the front door and once I crossed the threshold to the outside, I tossed them as high into the air as my arms would allow. Watching them float down to the street and settle in the dust released a catharsis inside me so powerful that without thinking, I walked back inside and took another armful. Again I threw them into the sky and decided I would not stop until all of my stories were liberated. However, when I went back for a third round, I realized the magnitude of this operation. There were piles and piles of signs and posters and flyers and leaflets, it would take all night for me to carry them away. I stumbled around a bit, thinking of a way to expedite the task at hand, and then aha! I remembered the cigar-smoking man and his torch-wielding lackey. I rummaged around the desks and soon I found it, a small blue lighter.

I started dumping all of the signs and posters into the biggest garbage can I could find, and once it was sufficiently full, I lit a small fire – a controlled burn! The fire burned bright, and as the ashes of theft drifted to the ceiling, I deposited more flyers and leaflets in their place. The flames rose high above the lid of the trash can and I watched as they licked the ceiling tiles, as if reaching out to scold them for their complicity in this crime. I felt at peace. The warmth of the fire swaddled me like a newborn baby, delivering a calm that I had not known for a long while.

How long was I frozen in this state of toasty nirvana? Ten seconds? Ten minutes? I cannot say for sure, but the next thing I knew, a wall of light flashed from outside and a voice shouted, Freeze! Jolted from my calm, I shouted back, Who is that?! And they replied, Freeze! Police! Walk out of the building with your hands up! There were still many stacks of papers to liberate, and I did not like the idea of leaving them hostage, but I am a law-abiding citizen, so I did as I was asked. I was sure that the police would understand once I explained the situation to them, but as soon as I emerged outside, they shoved me to the ground and held me in place as more and more vehicles with sirens wailing arrived. I wrenched my head back towards the building and saw that the fire had escaped the garbage can and had spread throughout the whole first floor. The building must not have had a proper sprinkler system. If only they had let me stay inside, I would have been able to make sure the fire was safely contained!

As the firefighters battled the blaze, the police lifted me off the ground and threw me into the back of their car. I told them that I had committed no crime and this could all be cleared up, but they insisted that I go to the station and that I could tell my story there. I did not think that was ideal, but like I said I have respect for our city officials, so I complied. From there it was holding cells, police interviews, and meetings with frazzled lawyers. Not the ideal way to get the full story if you ask me.

And so, ladies and gentlemen of the jury, that is why I am here today. A simple misunderstanding! I was only in that office to take back what was stolen from me, and I think you will agree that my actions were completely reasonable and within the law. I hope to get back to my shop as soon as possible, the school year has already begun and based on what I am hearing the people at LessonMax have gotten off to a rocky start without me. I need to get in contact with Mayor O'Malley as well, he said he would send over the contact to produce lessons with the LessonMax team, but my cousin has been checking my mail every day and he says it has not yet arrived. I'm sure we will sort all that out soon.

So, your honor, did that answer your question? It did not? What was the question again? Ah yes, I swear to tell the truth the whole truth and nothing but the truth, I do swear. Now let's get on to the next question. There are some details I left out from my previous answer, and I would like to make sure the story is complete.

Vodkas and Gins

Write and Wrong Cocktail Lounge Specials

In Search of Lost Thyme
10 oz gin

5 oz lemon juice

5 oz simple syrup

30 oz Champagne

Garnish with a lemon and a dozen sprigs of thyme

Serve in seven glasses

Infinite Zest
2 oz Grey Goose vodka

3 oz fresh squeezed lemonade

1/2 oz. raspberry liqueur

A twist of lemon zest, orange zest, lime zest, grapefruit zest, kumquat zest, pomelo zest, citron zest, mandarin orange zest, clementine zest, Meyer lemon zest, and blood orange zest

Crushed ice

Garnish with a frozen honeydew melon ball

Serve with endnotes

War and Peach
2 oz vodka

1 oz cognac

4 oz Lemonade

1 oz Simple Syrup

Garnish with a sliced peach

Serve philosophically

The Adventures of Huckleberry Gin
2 oz gin

0.5 oz triple sec

1 oz huckleberry simple syrup

1 oz lemon juice

3 oz club soda

Ice cubes

Garnish with frozen huckleberries

Serve with cunning

The Old Man and the Seagrams
2 oz Seagrams gin

2 oz Ocean Spray cranberry juice

1 oz lemon Juice

Ice Cubes

Garnish with fresh cranberries and mint leaves

Serve stoically

Sing, Unberried, Sing

Infuse vodka with strawberries, blueberries, raspberries, and blackberries for 24 hours

Strain berries from vodka

Mix 2 oz of infused vodka with 6 oz soda water

Garnish with a lime slice

Serve with lots of ice

The Picture of Dorian Grey Goose

1.5 oz Grey Goose vodka

2 oz sparkling white wine

1 oz elderflower liqueur

1 oz fresh lemon juice

Garnish with a mint sprig and an orange slice

Serve from a fountain of youth

Their Eyes Were Watching Vodka

2 oz vodka

1 oz Aperol

2 oz grapefruit juice

1 oz simple syrup

Garnish with an orange slice

Serve liberated

Go Tell It on the Mountain Dew

2 oz gin

1 oz Mountain Dew Code Red

1/2 teaspoon Maraschino liqueur

2 pineapple chunks

Garnish with Mountain Dew candy

Serve coy

3

Context Clues

On the morning of the first day of school, Chris stood outside of Cayetano Coll y Cuchí Middle School and took two deep breaths. Ever since he was young, he had longed to leave Wisconsin, and now here he was. Only 150 miles away, but in a different world. Growing up in Baraboo was a bore; college in Beloit was a step in the right direction, but it still felt like he was only a nanometer from home; then finally, one major, two minors, a certificate, a temporary teaching license, and a profoundly annoyed career services department later, he had made it to Chicago. A shoebox of an apartment in Lakeview, a hooptie street-parked precariously, and a job teaching middle school math in Humboldt Park. He was ready to teach some algebra and change some lives.

The first week hit Chris like a runaway toboggan. Sure, he had been a diligent student in his education classes, and done his fourteen weeks of student teaching in South Beloit, but none of that prepared him for the feeling of standing in front of that desk and watching 30 teenagers flood into his classroom. *His* classroom. He had his lesson plans down pat, and was even able to run his contingency plans by Principal Roth-Ramirez during staff week, but when school started for real, he flubbed his jokes and forgot their names and after four days, he had only gotten through two full lessons with each class. He even stayed late one day to cut out big bubble letters that spelled out "Mr. Krause" to paste to the board at the front of the classroom so the kids would remember how to say his name right. They had called him "Mr. Claus" and "Mr. Close" and "Mr. Kraut" – pretty much everything *except* his name.

Even worse, adjusting to Chicago had been more challenging that Chris expected. He had hoped that by the end of the summer he would have an exciting and diverse group of friends that would go to cool concerts and eat at underground restaurants. He wanted his life in the city to be real, not like the fluffy stuff you see in all the TV shows. And sure, he had made a few friends in his building, but they were mostly Midwest transplants like himself and he barely got around to exploring the city beyond all the touristy places he went with his parents when they came to visit in August. The whole trip they had pestered him about moving to Chicago, asking why he wanted to go all the way to another state to teach, why he didn't want to stay in Wisconsin where parking was abundant and the school yards stretched into the horizon, only ending where the dairy farms began. They didn't understand that he wanted to work where the schools really needed him. He tried to explain it to them, but then his mom would ask about crime and his uncle would make an ethnicity-based joke and then Chris would change the subject.

When school prep started in the summer, Chris tried to make friends with the other young teachers, but most of them already knew each other, so it was hard to break in. Most days he sat next to Mr. Montoya, one of the Spanish teachers, and they seemed to get along well. By the end of the week, he thought they might even be friends. But once the school year started, he would only see Mr. Montoya in passing, and never found a good time to see if he wanted to grab a drink or catch a game. Plus, they called each other by Mr. and Ms. so much that he kept forgetting Mr. Montoya's first name. Roberto, maybe? He would look into that.

More pressing were his classes. Only one week in and they were already behind. That first weekend, he lay awake in bed thinking of how he would get them back on track. By Monday morning, he felt like he had a plan for all of his classes but one. Sixth period, eighth grade Algebra. The material was challenging and the students were a bit rusty from the summer. That alone would be a challenge, but there was another major roadblock in his way. That roadblock's name was Javier Garcia.

On the first day of classes, Chris had planned for fifteen minutes of getting-to-know-you name-games with the class, and Javier by himself had taken eight minutes giving fake names and insisting that he was a direct descendant of Kublai Khan and next in line to be the Khagan-Emperor of Mongolia. He had asked to be called J-Glizzy, Abu Dhabi Javy, The Abscission of Division, El Mago, Usain Humbolt, West Side Willy, DJ Arroz con Pollo, and Juan Hancock before Chris was finally able to get him to settle on 'Javy'. Clever kid with a defiant streak and a big vocabulary – a dangerous combination.

By sixth period on Friday, Chris was depleted. Class started well enough; everyone got into groups smoothly and worked on math problems, even the lecture went off without a hitch. But once they got back into groups for more work time, Javy decided the class had gone too long without a disruption. It started small, him talking loudly to his groupmates about something clearly non-math related. Then when Chris walked over to ask him to get back on task, he brushed him off and continued talking and laughing intentionally too loud. Chris asked him again, and again Javy ignored him. Chris decided it was time to make a statement.

He had been back-talked and side-talked and get-out-of-my-face-talked a dozen times this week so far, many times by Javy himself, but hadn't pushed the issue to a detention or behavior report. All the books he had read said to start strict at the beginning of the school year, otherwise the kids would walk all over him and he'd never be able to regain control. He had asked Mr. Montoya what he thought, and he told him that Chris needed the class to know that he was not to be pushed around, that they would all be learning math this year whether they liked it or not. So when Javy ignored him that second time, Chris looked him dead in the eyes and said, "Javier Garcia, if you don't quiet down and get back on task, there will be severe consequences!"

His stern tone sucked all the air out of the room, and for a few seconds, an eerie silence hung over the class. Then, without breaking eye contact, Javy stood up and laughed directly into Chris's face. "Ja-VEE-er Gar-SEE-ah," Javy said with a mocking voice, "if you don't quiet down RiGHt nOw there will be sEVeRe CoNSeQuEncEs" Switching back to his regular voice he continued, "Get out of here, Mr. Krause. It's Friday, I'm not doing that shit." The class exploded in laughter. Chris's face turned beet red. This was not going well, but he couldn't back down now.

"That's it! I'm writing you up and your parents will be getting a call home this afternoon about your behavior. Now get back to work or you'll be going to Principal Roth-Ramirez's office." The class let out a long *ooooooo* in unison and Javy slinked down into his chair.

"Whatever Mr. Krause." He grabbed for his paper and started scribbling down letters and numbers. Chris walked slowly back to his desk and sat in his chair. Surveying the classroom, all the other students seemed to have returned to their work, unfazed by what had just occurred. The rest of the period went by without incident, maybe he had not completely blown it.

When the bell rang and all the students were on their way to their next class, Chris logged onto his laptop and opened the student roster. He navigated to Javy's name and clicked on the Parent/ Guardian tab. Only one record: Mother – Jaslene Garcia. Chris leaned back and thought to himself. Maybe Javy just had the first week of school jitters. Chris knew he had two younger siblings in elementary school, it must be difficult being the oldest of three kids with a single mother. Maybe he was stressed because he had to help get his siblings ready for school while Mom rushed off to work in the morning. Maybe he had some unresolved father issues to work through. He decided to give Javy a break this time. He could always call his mom next week if the behavior continued.

When school let out, Chris went outside to watch dismissal besides the school's front doors. Principal Roth-Ramirez saddled up next to him. "How'd your first week go Mr. Krause?"

"It was okay. Some highs, some lows."

"Hey, you're still here, count that as a victory."

"Still here because I didn't get fired? Or because I didn't quit?"

Principal Roth-Ramirez just shrugged and looked out over the bedlam of parents and children. Chris scanned the line of cars and a woman in dark blue scrubs standing next to a small sedan caught his eye. She had dark wavy hair and eyes that were weary but arresting. The scrubs clung close to her body, ruffling around her curves. A shiver shot up his spine.

"Principal Roth-Ramirez, how many of these parents do you think you know?"

"Most of the 7th and 8th grade, I'm working on the 6th."

"Who's that over there by the SUV?"

"What is this, quiz bowl?"

"Just asking."

"That's a 6th grader's parent, Emily Velasquez I think, she wouldn't be in your classes."

"She is not. What about that dad over there in the jeans?"

"Some uncle I think, picking up the Santoyo boys."

"Mateo is in my math class."

"That he is."

"What about that woman in the scrubs over by the sedan?"

"That would be your friend Javy Garcia's mom." Chris could feel his stomach drop. "I believe you and him are getting acquainted already."

"We are, we are."

"I've actually never talked with her though, she's kind of hard to get a hold of. And speak of the devil himself..."

In the grass in front of the school, a group of boys were arguing about some internet video. Javy was loudly insisting it was real, and as the other boys retorted, his voice grew from a yip to a shout. Chris looked at Principal Roth-Ramirez, "I'll let him know his mom is here."

"Thanks Mr. Krause."

Chris slowly walked over and the conversation and the boys fell to a hush. "Javy, can I speak with you for a second?" The other boys glanced around.

"Umm, sure, okay." They took a few steps away from the group.

"Hey Javy, I just wanted to say I'm sorry if I lost my temper a bit today. I didn't mean to yell at you."

"Oh, umm, it's okay Mr. Krause. I was acting a fool, I deserved it."

"You're a smart kid Javy, I hope we can have a good year together."

"Okay."

"You mom is in the pickup line by the way, you shouldn't keep her waiting."

"Yes, Mr. Krause."

Javy looked back at his friends and gave them all a nod, then walked over to the line of cars and got into the sedan with his mom.

Chris went back to his classroom and decided to get some grading out of the way so he didn't have to take any papers home. He went through the quizzes he gave to the 8th graders; lots of sloppy writing and calculation mistakes, but overall not too shabby. When he got to Javy's quiz he knew from the first question that it was going to be rough. Most of the questions only had a few scribbles of work on them, none of them had a full answer, and some of them he didn't even attempt at all. Not a great start to the school year. He rolled the paper in his hands and thought that it would probably be best to call Javy's mom to make sure she was aware of his struggles with the content. Plus, now that he thought about it, a quick chat about the behavior couldn't hurt. Nothing punitive, just a routine check-in. It made sense to get in touch with her anyway, since it seemed like Javy was going to need some extra support, it would be best to develop a relationship, a professional relationship, to make sure Javy had every chance to succeed.

Chris opened his laptop and navigated back to the student information system. He clicked into Javy's name, then into the Parent/Guardian tab. He took out his cell phone and dialed Jaslene Garcia's phone number. Chris waited as the tone pulsed, and pulsed, and pulsed…and then sent him to voicemail. Realizing he was not prepared to leave a voicemail, he quickly hung up and put his phone back on his desk. He would try again in five or ten minutes. But before he had a chance, his phone buzzed with excitement. A text from the number he just called.

Hello Mr. Krause this is Javys Mom. Javy told me that he act up in class today and want 2 say that he is very sorry and he try harder next week 2 be good in class. I will talk 2 him about him act up.

Chris read it over three times, thought, then responded.

Hi Jaslene! Thanks for the text! I'm glad Javy told you. He was a little disruptive today, but I think it's just the first week jitters. It would be great to speak with you so we can talk about expectations for Javy in Algebra, are you free anytime this weekend for a quick call?

Hello Mr Krause text is better my english no good. I like to type on phone.

Got it, sure thing! I want to make sure he's getting extra help with math if he needs it. We had our first quiz and he seems to be struggling with the material.

Yes Javy forget math over the summer this happens every year.

Got it, that is very common. I will keep you updated with his progress.

Yes of course thank you Mr Krause

Have a great weekend! Tell Javy to have a fun weekend too, because on Monday we get back to work!

Yes of course, thank you Mr Krause

You are very welcome!

Chris put his phone down and leaned back in his chair. He picked his phone up again to see if any more texts came in, put it back down, then picked it back up and saved Jaslene's phone number to his contacts. The seeds of a very productive parent-teacher relationship had been planted. A sheepish grin emerged on his face.

— — —

Javy gazed out the window as his mom drove them west on Division Street. He missed Diego. This was the first time they wouldn't be at the same school since 4th grade. When Diego first told him that he was going far away for school, Javy thought he meant Wilmette or something. Not Iowa. They hadn't talked or texted or called or anything since he left. Diego said the boarding school he was going to didn't allow cell phones and kids couldn't even get letters or emails for the first few months. Javy didn't understand why Diego's mom even made him go to school out there, those schools were usually for kids who got in trouble and Diego only got detention like once or twice a month. It was usually for something funny too, like re-arranging the desks before class started or switching names with other kids when they had a sub. The classrooms felt empty without him.

Javy had other friends at school, but not friends like Diego. With the other kids, he still had to be on his guard. They would hang out at lunch and mess around in class, but then one of them would go too far and Javy would get pissed off, but there was nowhere to go and if he got mad at them it would just make it worse. He wished he hadn't gone off on Mr. Krause in class today. He was trying to get one of his friends to get mad and do something stupid so that they would get in trouble and be the first one to make a scene in class, but he ended up just getting himself worked up and now Mr. Krause would put a target on him.

Javy put his temple against the window and felt the vibration of the car shake his head. If he opened his mouth slightly and made a soft *uhhhhh* sound the car would bounce his jaw and it would make an *ubba-ubba-ubba-ubba* sound that he liked. He wondered what they did all day at Diego's school. *Ubba-ubba-ubba-ubba.* Then he put his ear to the window and all he could hear was a blur until his mom smacked him on the side of the neck, bringing his head off the window, and all the noise back into focus.

"Papi, give me my phone back." Javy fumbled with her phone.

"One second, I'm finishing a level on Potato Party."

"Javy, now." Javy quickly navigated back to the text messages and deleted the conversation with Mr. Krause before handing the phone over. "Who was that who called?"

"Looked like spam."

"Typical."

The next morning, Javy's Mom had to work at the hospital, so Javy was left to roam. He set out east on Grand Ave and made his way to Rufino Park, the neighborhood hub for bored youth. When he got there, the only people he saw were a group of high school guys who were sometimes cool to him, depending on their mood. They thought they were a real clique, called themselves the Rufino K-Pops; repping the streets between the train tracks and Pulaski Road that all started with the letter K. There was Kilborne then Kostner then Kolin then Kildare, Keeler then Kevdale then Karlov then Keystone. Come through the Ks and you'll get popped, they would say. Javy didn't think that any of those guys had ever even held a gun, but he still tread lightly.

The K-Pops always gave Javy shit because he lived on Tripp. The only street in their neighborhood that didn't start with K. He thought about turning around, but one of the K-Pops saw him and called out, "Yo Lil Tripp! Come here." Javy trudged over. "Where's your moms at today?"

"She's working."

"What you on? I know you got some of those middle school hoes you can invite over."

Javy kicked the dirt. Another one of the guys chimed in.

"P, man, look at him, you know Trippy here gets no girl."

"Cero gatas."

"He's more solo than a cup at a white-boy party."

"Last time someone saw his dick they slapped his ass and said, *It's a boy!*"

Once they were finished laughing at their own jokes, the K-Pops turned to Javy.

"So where your girls at, little man?"

Javy looked up at the sky and scrunched his face. They were always pressing him about girls, who he's been with and who let him do what to their where. He used to have no problem hanging with the older crews. A few years ago, all the older guys seemed to care about was getting spray paint to tag the building by the tracks and how many bags of chips they could swipe from the corner store before the owner told their parents. But then, everything became about girls. Sure, he wasn't grossed out by girls like he was in elementary school, but these guys seemed to have nothing on their mind but figuring out how to see as many girls naked as possible. He didn't get it. Diego didn't either. Javy wasn't sure what the other guys at Coll y Cuchí thought, but if he asked they might start making fun of him too. When he saw the K-Pops at the park a few weeks ago, they showed him a video on their phone and laughed when he turned his head away. They asked him where his boyfriend was and then shooed him away. One of the K-Pops punched him on his shoulder.

"Tripp, what you got to say?"

Javy clenched his hands behind his back. "I get what I get." The K-Pops cracked up.

"Oh, so you a philosopher now! Get your ass out of here."

Javy walked back home and avoided Rufino Park for the rest of the weekend.

On Monday, Mr. Krause seemed to have a little extra pep in his step. He was very friendly to Javy, saying hello like a million times and asking him how his weekend was. He even asked him how his mom was doing and mentioned that he had spoken with her over the weekend. Javy asked what his mom said, just to see what he would say, but Mr. Krause was being coy and didn't really answer.

As the week went on, Javy waxed and waned. Math was better now that Mr. Karuse was nice to him, but he put him in an assigned seat all the way on the other side of the room from his friends, so when they had to do group work, he was always stuck with the randos who were sitting next to him. On Thursday night after dinner, Javy asked his mom if he could borrow her phone to play Potato Party.

Hello Mr Krause how are you

Hello! I'm doing well, how about you?

Good good. I have a question. Could it be possible for Javy to sit next to his friends in math class? He say that he does good work with his friends and he sit all the way on the other side and he no does group work good with kids he dont know.

Hmmm. Let me think about it. He has been doing great this week!

Okay good thank you.

You're welcome Jaslene!

Javy wondered why Mr. Krause kept calling his mom by her first name like that. Adults are so weird. He saved Mr. Krause's phone number as *Coll y Cuchí Main Office* so he could find it easier next time, then deleted the text history and gave his mom back her phone.

Nothing changed on Friday, but the next Monday in math class, Mr. Krause got up in front of the class to make an announcement. "Hello everyone! How are y'all feeling today?" The class grumbled something resembling *good* in response. "Awesome! Well, we've had a great first two weeks, and I figured since you all have been so good about doing work and staying on task, if anyone wants to move seats we can switch from assigned to free choice. As long as everyone is able to behave!"

A hush fell over the class. Everyone gripped the edge of their desks, ready to make a dash for the seat of their choice. Their eyes fixated on Mr. Krause.

"Go ahead, switch if you'd like."

The class erupted in the rattling of chairs and squeaking of sneakers. Beelines were made and Javy was able to snag a seat in the back-left corner with his friends. When the class settled down, Mr. Krause proceeded with the day's lesson and Javy spent the rest of class hiding a devilish smirk.

That week in math class was a bit louder than normal, with everyone chatting with their friends during work time, but nothing that would raise any alarms until on Friday when Javy and his friends were discussing their weekend plans. One of his friends told him that he got invited to a high school party to dance bachata because some girls on his block saw him dancing bachata and told him that he was better than any of the guys at their high school at dancing bachata so they invited him to dance bachata with them, and Javy told his friend that he was bullshitting because Javy had seen him dance bachata and he looked like a worm with knees, and these girls must go to high school in Wyoming or maybe they go to the Stevie Wonder School for the Visually Impaired, because there is no way his knee-worm-having-ass was even the best bachata dancer in this very math class. Then they both got up to demonstrate their moves and Javy knocked over his chair and Mr. Krause stormed over and was not happy.

"Javy! This does not look like you're working on graphing functions."

"Sorry Mr. Krause, we were just–"

"Javy please, I let you all choose your seats because I trusted you, but I will go back to assigned seats if that's what you want."

"No I don't."

"Then act like it. Pick up your chair and get back to work." Javy's friends muzzled their laughs as Javy bent down to pick up his chair.

That night Javy was surfing the web in his room when his mom knocked on his door.

"Honey, did anything happen at school today?"

"Not really, why?"

"I got a strange text from the Main Office, I didn't even know I had their number in my phone, and when I tried to call back I got some cell phone's voicemail."

"That's weird." Shit, Javy thought, he forgot Mr. Krause might text his mom first. "What did the text say?"

"It said you were being disruptive in class."

"Oh."

"What happened?"

"I was being disruptive."

"Javy, what happened?"

"I was dancing and knocked over a chair."

"Papi, why were you dancing in math class?"

"Because I was bored."

"Javy…"

"Okay, because Ernie was telling us about this party he was going to and was trying to say that he was the best bachata dancer in the class but I know he's not so I had to show him but–"

"Javy, okay. Please just behave in class. I don't want the school texting me this nonsense."

"Yes mom."

"Thank you."

"But I already finished my math homework for the weekend! Can I use your phone to play games?"

"I have to make another call, but when I'm done."

"Thanks mom."

When Javy got his hands on his mom's phone, he navigated straight to the texts. There it was.

Hi Jaslene. We had another issue with Javy in class today, he was being very disruptive.

He saw his mom had called the number 45 minutes ago, thankfully Mr. Krause hadn't called back yet. He had to get out in front of this.

Hello Mr Krause sorry for the call I butt dial. I am sorry Javy was disrupt, I will talk with him about it this weekend.

Thanks Jaslene. He was great last week and so I let him sit next to his friends like you said, but this week he started losing focus and I want to make sure he's not falling behind.

Yes he say you let him sit with friends. Thank you thank you, he very happy about that.

Has he had trouble focusing in class before?

Yes sometime he get distracted. Some days school is easy for him but other days school no easy and he no listen.

I can see that. I'll try and give him some extra attention next week and see if it can help.

Thank you thank you Mr Krause.

You are very welcome!

Then, Javy decided to test his luck.

Oh also, Javy tell me that sometime he gets hungry at the end of the day but he say that they are not allowed to eat snacks after lunch so he hungry in math class and it harder to pay attention. Do you have any snacks you can give him? Hot chips are his favorite.

Oh wow, I didn't even realize. Let me check with Principal Roth-Ramirez because it would be awful if he's having trouble focusing because he's hungry. I think we can figure something out.

Thank you thank you Mr Krause!

Happy to help!

Javy deleted the texts then blocked Mr. Krause's number. He couldn't risk getting any more incoming texts or calls.

On Monday, Javy was walking in from recess when he saw Mr. Krause standing over by the door. Mr. Krause called out to him.

"Javy! Come here for a second."

"What?"

"Over *here* please."

"Okay."

"So I spoke with your mother this weekend."

"Okay."

"She said that sometimes it's hard for you to focus when you're hungry and that might be why you act up sometimes."

"Umm, maybe, I guess."

"So I got you something to help out." Mr. Krause pulled out a bag of hot chips from behind his back. "Eat these before class please. We need you full and ready to learn!"

Javy's eyes bulged. The chips! Trying to keep his cool, he took the bag gently.

"Oh, umm, thank you Mr. Krause."

"You're welcome, Javy. See you in class."

Javy stuffed the chips into his backpack and scurried into the building.

— — —

The next few weeks, Chris felt like he was really getting into his groove. Lesson plans flowed out of him and the days just rolled by. Even sixth period math was going smoothly. Mr. Montoya had taught him some fun Spanish phrases to pepper into the lessons, and he always got a good laugh out of the kids when he used them. The class engaged with the material, they had lively discussions and group work, and even Javy was getting settled. He would act up every now and then, but Chris kept a desk drawer full of gummy snacks and hot chips and he would sneak them to Javy when he had a good day. Positive reinforcement seemed to be working.

Chris wanted to let Javy's mom know about his progress, but when he texted, she never seemed to respond. The messages weren't even getting delivered. One Friday, he pulled Javy aside after class and asked if his mom's phone was working. Javy gave him an odd look.

"I think so, why?"

"I just wanted to let her know how great you've been doing in class!"

"Oh, umm, okay. I'll let her know, maybe something is up with her phone."

"Thanks Javy! Off you go." Javy scurried out of the classroom and at dismissal that day, Chris made sure to be out by the line of cars to see if he could see Jaslene. Sure enough, when Javy broke away from his friends at pick up, she was standing outside her car like usual. Chris caught her eye and gave a friendly wave. She gave him a faint wave back. As Javy ran into her arms, she wrapped him in a big hug. She must be so tired from a long day at work, Chris thought. How attractive it was for her to still have the energy to love her son so dearly. What a strong woman.

That night at home, Chris sat eating dinner and scrolling on his phone when a notification popped up. A text from Jaslene Garcia. His thumb trembled as it hovered over the phone. He should wait, play it cool. He didn't want her to think he had been waiting for her to text him from the moment Javy got in the car. He was a cool guy who did cool things and didn't answer texts the second they came in. But! He was also a caring teacher who would drop everything at a moment's notice for his students if they needed him to. What if it was urgent? That's crazy, what would be urgent at 6:48pm on a Friday evening? But what if it *was* urgent? He picked his phone back up, then put it back down. Maybe he would read it, then decide when to answer. But what if she could see that he read her text and didn't respond? Did her phone have that capability? Did *his* phone have that capability? What kind of phone did she have? Chris picked the phone back up and went to his text messages. He would do it. He would read the text and respond promptly. Who cares if that didn't make him cool. He cared about his students and a mature woman like Jasline would appreciate that.

Chris had been trying to work on his impulsivity recently – trying to be more impulsive, that is. He had always been so deliberate, everything was planned out. He regretted how he wasted the summer with his inaction. He should have gone to that street fest! Talked to those people! Now that he was a city man, he needed to be able to act at a moment's notice. Every morning in the shower he would practice by getting the water temperature just right and then standing under the water, feeling like he was wrapped up in a warm cocoon, till he felt his absolute most comfortable. Then, he would suddenly grab the faucet handle and slam the shower off. Standing there naked and dripping, shivering in the cold air, he would feel one step closer to the man of action he knew he would be.

So as his thumb quivered over her text message, Chris decided that this was time for action as well. He opened the text message.

Hello Mr Krause. Javy say today that my phone not get message that you send? I very sorry sometime I have to turn my phone on and off because it expensive to keep on all the time.

Chris read the text four times. Should he wait? Maybe he should wait. Let her dwell on what he would say a bit. But no, he was a man of action, remember? He would text her back promptly. He started to type, then deleted what he wrote, then started again, then deleted again. A man of action still must send the best texts, it would be crazy to rush and be left with mediocrity. He realized that Jaslene might be able to see him typing in the box, so he moved to his notepad app and spent a few minutes crafting his response. After a few more false starts, he scrapped all he had written, and decided to play it cool in this first text. Simple, clean.

Hello Jaslene! Not a problem, I completely understand. Thanks for letting me know.

Chris held his breath as he hit send and immediately saw the typing bubbles pop up on Jaslene's side of the text. Then they stopped. Then they started again. Then they stopped. She must be thinking of what to text him as well. A smile crept across Chris's face. A few seconds later, a new text popped up.

In future if you need to send me anything you can tell Javy and he will tell me then I can text you first. No need to call or text because my phone is usually off and it would be bad for you to call or text.

Sounds great, I will be sure to do that!

Since that night, Chris had been looking for reasons to text with Jaslene, but much to his surprise, when they got back the next week, Javy was quiet and undisruptive. He followed directions, worked quietly with his group, and could barely squeak out a thank you when Chris rewarded him with snacks. It was a bit disconcerting, but then again, class had never been better. Chris figured he'd take what he could get.

Everything was going smoothly until one Friday when the class was doing group work and Javy's group was goofing off. Everyone in the group but Javy, that is, who was sitting sullen in the corner. The boys in his group would tease and prod, and Javy rebuffed their every attempt, until one of them booped him in the head with a ruler and Javy snatched the ruler and proceeded to break it over his friend's head. The class all turned to watch as the boys lunged at each other, but luckily Chris had been keeping his eye on them and was able to break it up before they threw any punches. Standing between them, he shouted for them to settle down and Javy stormed off into the hallway. The other boy calmly picked the ruler bits out of his hair and softly whined about how he didn't even do anything.

Once the class was settled Chris went into the hallway to look for Javy and found him sitting next to the water fountain. He crouched next to him.

"Javy, are you okay?"

"Yeah yeah, I'm fine."

"When you're ready–"

"I'll come back to class and apologize. I know."

"And when you–"

"Yeah yeah, I'll tell my mom to text you."
"Thank you Javy."

Chris needed some advice. He looked for Mr. Monotoya in the teacher lounge, but didn't see him, so he walked to his classroom and didn't see him there either. Back in the teachers' lounge, another teacher suggested getting Principal Roth-Ramirez involved, but Chris decided to see if he could have a conversation with Jaslene first. Maybe they could figure something out.

Chris waited all night and no texts arrived. He was disappointed, he wanted to talk with Jaslene. It pained him that he couldn't reach out first. As he brushed his teeth he looked into the mirror and wondered what kind of men Jaslene was attracted to. Tall and buff? Slender and suave? What did Javy's father look like? What did Javy's father *act* like? Chris poked at his stomach, which had just started to soften this year. Not that he worked out or anything, but he ate well and was active and nature blessed him with a good metabolism, so the base was there. Maybe he should start doing crunches. His chest had some nice definition, his arms too. He could never tell about his face. He knew he wasn't horrific and he knew he wasn't gorgeous, but he could never place himself in the funny-looking to normal-looking to nice-looking spectrum. Especially now that he was in Chicago. Back in Wisconsin, he generally has success getting dates, benefiting greatly from, as they would joke, the lack of a global talent pool. But Chicago was a whole new world. Big thick hunks of hunk, smartly-dressed doctors, Latin Lovers, Aesthetic Asians, was there a non-offensive way to describe attractive Black men? Chris thought about it…player? Could he say player? Probably not. Super fly? Maybe 50 years ago.

Chris was brushing his teeth all the while, and the toothpaste foam had gathered in his mouth to the point where his lips could no longer keep in the foamy mass. Just as he realized this his respiratory tract buckled, and he coughed up all the foam right onto his bathroom mirror. After a deep sigh, he wiped it all into the sink and called it a night.

As he sat down on his bed, he checked his phone and saw a new text from Jaslene. His heart skipped. He hit the lights, tucked himself in, and opened his phone.

Hello Mr Krause. Javy say you want to text to me?

Hi Jaslene! Yes, Javy and one of his friends got into a small fight in math class today and I just wanted to check in to make sure you knew about it.

Yes he tell me. Javy is very sorry. He has been having very tough week.

I noticed. He has been quiet all week in class, didn't really seem like himself. Is everything okay?

Yes maybe

Did something happen?

Yes but it not a big deal. Javy okay.

Even small things can become big issues. If Javy is having a tough time, we have a social worker at Coll y Cuchí he can talk to if he wants.

It okay. Some older kids in the neighborhood mess with Javy and it make him feel bad.

Oh no, that's awful. I'm so sorry to hear that. Did they hurt him?

No, but they take his shoes and throw them over the street wires.

That is so awful. I'm so very sorry for Javy. That must have been such a shock, no wonder he's been quiet all week.

Yes, I think he quiet because of the shoes. Going outside in neighborhood is less fun for Javy now.

I can imagine. He must be so scared.

Javy not scared. It just less fun for him so he no want to do it.

Of course. Would it be okay if I tell Principal Roth-Ramirez? I think she might be able to help in this situation.

No please do not. Javy do not want anyone to know. I only tell you because I trust you

Okay, you have my trust. I will keep it between us.

Thank you Mr Krause. You are a nice man Javy is glad to have you as teacher

We're lucky to have him in our class.

Thank you Mr Krause you very nice. I go to bed now goodnight

Good night Jaslene!

The next day, everything seemed back to normal in class. Javy was semi-disruptive as usual, but acquiesced when Chris asked him to quiet down. After the period ended Chris asked Javy to stay for a minute. Javy's friends laughed and Javy looked annoyed as he dragged his feet over to Chris's desk.

"Javy, I spoke with you mom last night."

"Okay."

"She told me about what happened last week."

"What happened last week?"

"With the kids in your neighborhood."

"What?"

"She told me about they took your shoes and…"

"Who took my shoes?"

"She said that they threw them over the power wires."

"Mr. Krause, I have no idea what you're talking about."

"Javy…"

"What?"

"You're wearing different shoes this week. What happened to your old shoes?"

"So I got new shoes, okay?"

"Those aren't new, they're all beat up."

"So I got OLD shoes, who cares?! Mr. Krause, no one took my shoes."

"Are you saying your mom was lying to me?"

"My mom is not a liar!" Don't say that shit about my mom!"

"I'm not–"

"Don't say that shit about my mom."

"It's just–"

"Can I go?"

"Javy…."

"Can I go?!"

"Yes."

Javy stood up fast, throwing his chair backwards, and stormed out of the room.

———

Javy stomped through the hallway. He knew he shouldn't have acted that way to Mr. Krause, but he panicked and that's what came out. What was Mr. Krause expecting? To surprise him like that after class, he should have at least let him know beforehand. Whatever, it was over. Javy was already late to history class, so he figured it wouldn't make a big difference if he stopped by the computer lab for a few minutes. He told the teacher at the desk that Ms. Romero sent him over to print something out and the teacher shrugged as he opened a laptop and pulled up his email account. He had already sent like a thousand emails to Diego and hadn't gotten any back, but that must mean they didn't let Diego write emails because he would never leave him hanging like that. Maybe they let him read emails but not write them, he hoped at least. Javy hammered out a quick email about how he snuck in the computer lab and all the other dumb stuff going on at Coll y Cuchí, then shit the laptop and slipped out of the computer lab and back to history class.

That night after dinner, he borrowed his mom's phone, unblocked Mr. Krause's number, and started texting.

> *Mr Krause Javy wants to say he is sorry for how he behaved today after class. He knows you are trying to help but he was surprised and didn't know how to act. He is very sorry.*

> *Hello Jaslene! I completely understand. It was out of nowhere, I understand why he might have been freaked out.*

> *Yes he was just freak out. He thank you for asking and I think he just needs time on his own.*

> *Totally. Like I said, I'm always here for him.*

The next day, as math class ended, Javy stopped by Mr. Krause's desk. "Hey Mr. Krause, do you have a second?"

"Sure Javy, what's up?"

"I didn't get this problem on the homework."

"Which one?"

"Umm, question 7a."

"Hmm, 7a…"

"And 7b and 7c."

"Yes, yes, that would follow. Here pull up a chair."

Javy sat down and he worked through the problem with Mr. Krause. He still didn't totally get it, but he kind of understood the answers, he was pretty sure at least. Sometimes in class when Mr. Krause was going over a problem he zoned out for a second and then when he got back to listening he was lost and the rest of the problem didn't make any sense. He could usually figure out most of the worksheets that Mr. Krause gave for homework, but it was nice having Mr. Krause explain it step-by-step to him.

"Thanks Mr. Krause." Javy said as he packed up his bookbag.

"You're very welcome. I'm glad you asked. Do you want a pass to your next class?"

"No thanks, I'm always late to history anyway, Ms. Felani doesn't mind."

From then on, Javy would stay after class once or twice a week and they would go over the homework and class problems that Javy didn't get. They would share a bag of hot chips and work through the problems. In class, Javy still goofed around, but he and Mr. Krause fell into a rhythm, and an unspoken line had been agreed upon that he never crossed. With his stellar behavior and solid grades, there wasn't much reason for Mr. Krause to text his mom. But once a week or so Javy would still send a text, at first just to check in on how Javy was doing in class, but soon it became friendly and they would joke about the school, Principal Roth-Ramirez, and Mr. Krause's so-called country ways.

One day after school, as they drove home, Javy's mom asked him if he liked his math teacher.

"He's cool, why?"

"He's a bit shy, no?"

"I guess, what do you mean?"

"Everytime I see him at pickup he gives me this big wave and stupid smile, but he never says anything."

"Oh yeah, he's like that I guess."

"He's not weird in class with you or any of the kids, right?"

"No, no. He's a good teacher."

"Okay good, can never be too careful these days. My friend Sandra was telling me about this teacher at her kid's school in Orland Park who got one of the kids phone numbers and they were exchanging inappropriate messages and it became this whole thing when…" Javy ears started ringing and it felt like his mom had put a vice around his stomach and was tightening it with each word of the story.

He knew it was bad to pretend to be his mom when he texted Mr. Krause, but everything seemed to work out, so he didn't think about it much at first. Every time he texted, he knew it was a little wrong, but it just felt like a little. Now all those littles were piling up and with his mom talking about what happened to other teachers, it started to feel big. It needed to end. He could just stop sending the texts, keep Mr. Krause's number blocked and see if it could last the rest of the year. But Mr. Krause always wanted to text his mom to say how good of a job he was doing and there were end-of-year teacher conferences. If he just stopped cold, Mr. Krause might try to call again or contact his mom another way. Javy thought long and hard, and decided it would be best if Javy told him himself. It would be the mature thing to do. Sure, Mr. Krause might be mad, but if he came clean, maybe he would go easy on him. Maybe he wouldn't even tell his mom.

Only thing was, Javy could not figure out how to tell him. Over text felt wrong, and every time he saw Mr. Krause in person, his stomach clenched and his jaw locked up. It felt like his body was trying to make sure the words never left his mouth. He kept a low profile in class and still met with Mr. Krause after, but Mr. Krause always looked so happy, and each time Javy figured that it could wait for another day.

The Friday before Spring Break, Javy decided that this was it. He could not keep living like this, Mr. Krause had to know the truth. He waited until after class, but other students were hanging around, and as Mr. Krause was sweeping them out of the classroom, Javy got caught in the swarm. In the hallway, Mr. Krause power walked away and Javy ran to catch up with him.

"Mr. Krause! Mr. Krause!"

"What is it Javy? I'm late for a meeting." Mr. Krause kept walking full steam.

"Mr. Krause, I have to tell you something." Javy could barely keep up.

"What is it?"

"It's umm, well umm…"

"Javy I really have to–"

"You know about how you and my mom text about me in school and stuff?"

"Yeah."

"And how she likes to text because she said she doesn't speak English that well?"

"Yes Javy, she told me."

"Okay, well…umm, so…" Mr. Krause abruptly stopped in front of a classroom. Two other teachers were standing outside.

"Javy, I really have to get to this meeting, is this urgent?" The other two teachers paused their conversation to listen in. The others already in the classroom glanced over as well.

"Umm, no but, she just wanted me to tell you that she thinks you're a really good teacher." Javy couldn't do it. Not in front of other teachers.

"Aww, that's very kind of her, Javy. Tell her I said I'm happy to do it for such a great kid like yourself."

Mr. Krause gave Javy an avuncular pat on the head, then slipped into the classroom. The other two teachers followed and shut the door behind them.

———

Chris walked into the Math Department meeting and plopped down in the back. They were meant to plan the last two months of the school year, the *final push* as the department head was calling it, like they were all gestating a baby together and labor would start after break. She went over lesson plans and curriculum, but Chris's head was elsewhere. Specifically, with Jaslene Garcia. For the first time in Chicago, he felt a real connection with someone. Sure, they only texted and exchanged coy waves at pickup time, but he could feel them growing closer. He daydreamt of taking her out to dinner, giggling as they exchanged choppy sentences, him in broken Spanish and her in broken English. They would start slow, for sure, it would be improper to move too quickly with a student's parent, but once it got to summer they could be free to spend more time together. Javy would be angry about it at first, what kid wouldn't? But Chris would chip away at his resistance with kindness and generosity, and slowly they would develop a bond. Not like father and son, Chris would always know his place in their blended family, but like uncle and nephew. A relationship based on mutual respect, not authority. Chris would take them up to Wisconsin to Lake Geneva and Door County and show Javy the Midwest outside Chicago. Jasleen would take him to Puerto Rico and they would sit on the beach in San Juan, soaking up the sun and laughing about how easily Chris's skin turned beet red. It could be a beautiful life. But he had to make the first move. She didn't take phone calls, so that was out of the question, and she didn't strike him as a woman who would appreciate being asked out over text messages. A letter maybe? But that felt too formal, too rigid. It would have to be in person, which meant it would have to be at pick-up. He would think of what he wanted to say, get it translated into Spanish, then ask her out when he had the chance. It would be smooth, but appropriate. Restrained, but romantic. Chris would have to thread the needle, but he had nine long days of Spring Break to figure that out. He would get started that night.

The school bell rang and the meeting wrapped, the staff fanned out across the school to shoo the kids out of the building and off school property as quickly as they could. Once the kids were good and gone, all the teachers gathered at Dabrowski's Bar for a start-of-break celebration. After a few rounds, Chris saw Mr. Montoya and figured this would be a great time to get his translator on board.

"Mr. Montoya!"

"Oh, hey Chris. What's up?"

"Happy Spring Break!"

"Yes yes, happy Spring Break to you too."

"So Mr. Montoya–"

"Hey so the kids aren't here, you can just call me Rob."

"Oh, sorry Rob."

"All good, what were you saying?"

"Ah, yes. So I have a translation project I might need some help on. Any chance you have a few hours at the end of break?"

"Umm, yeah maybe. What do you need translated?"

"Just a quick letter, a page or two tops."

"What kind of letter?"

"Umm…"

"What is it, a love letter or something?"

"Not exactly but–"

"But what?"

"It's embarrassing to say out loud."

"Sounds like it."

"Please?"

"Who is it to? Or is that even more embarrassing."

"Kinda."

"How about this, I'll translate the letter for you if you tell me who it's for."

"It's just, I really don't–"

"Your call."

"Okay, but you can't tell anyone."

"Your forbidden love is safe with me."

"I mean it, absolutely no one."

Rob smiled and zipped his lips with his thumb and pointer finger. Then he opened his mouth wide, pretended to throw the imaginary key down his throat, fake swallowed, and gave Chris a saucy wink. He wished he had another option, but time was of the essence and he had to get this done quickly. He would have to trust Rob.

Chris was planning to stick around the city for the week, but some last-minute pestering from his parents convinced him to trek back up to Wisconsin. There wasn't much in Chicago going on for him any-way, he figured the week in the sticks could be nice. He took the bus from Chicago to the Wisconsin Dells, and his mom was kind enough to pick him up from the god-forsaken fast-food parking lot where the bus dropped him off. On the ride back to his parents' house, his mom prodded him for the lurid details of his big city living. She asked if he was eating well (he wasn't), whether it was safe to walk at night in his neighborhood (it was), whether the students' parents ever brought tacos for the teachers (he wished). When they got back home, his father wrapped him up in a big bear hug, called him an eco-hippy freak, and led him back to his childhood bed where Chris dropped his bags and shut the door.

The week slipped by quickly. Chris spent his days loafing by the river, strolling through town, and helping his dad build his tool shed/man cave/time-out room in the backyard. A few of the kids he went to high school with were still around town, but no one that he really wanted to see, so he mostly kept to himself, wishing Jaslene would text. He turned that energy towards his letter, his speech. Every day he would draft new lines, cross them out, then draft them again. He only had one shot to ask her out for the first time, it had to be perfect. Their life together depended on it.

His last night in town, his parents took him out for dinner in Bara-boo. They wouldn't tell him the destination, just told him it would be a surprise and make him feel like he never left Chicago. Five minutes of driving later they arrived at Jose's Authentic Mexican Restaurant. Chris rubbed his face as they were led to their table.

"So Chrissy, what do you think? Just like *El Barrio* in Chicago?"

"Not quite Dad."

"But it's close?"

"Sure, it's close."

"Oh Dave, stop it. Chris, tell us more about Chicago. Any new friends we haven't heard about yet?"

"A few, some of the teachers and I hang out sometimes."

"What fun!"

"Any young ladies in your life?"

"Dave!"

"Well actually…"

"See! Go on son."

"Well there's a woman…and we're not *dating* dating yet, but we text a ton and we're going to start going out soon."

"How fun! What's her name."

"Oh–"

"Go on."

"It's Jaslene."

"Ooooo Jaslene!"

"How *e x o t i c*."

"Dad…"

"How did you meet this *J a s l e n e*?"

"We umm, well, she's actually the mom of one of my students."

"Chrissy you dog!"

"Is that allowed? What about the father?!"

"Well, there's no rules *against* it, as long as everything is disclosed and everything. And she separated from his father, he's not around."

"Oh that's so sad."

"Look at that, my Chrissy is going to be a step-dad! These kids, move to the big city and grow up so fast…"

"Well not as fast as some of Chris's friends from High School, did you hear about the youngest Schmidt girl? She's pregnant with her third kid already!"

"Umm, no–"

"Gotta watch out for those Schmidt girls, you'll get them pregnant just by lookin' at 'em!"

Chris sunk into his chair as his dad cackled and his mom went on gabbing about the Baraboo kids Chris's age and their various accomplishments and misdeeds. He noticed the clanking of the restaurant kitchen and when the door swung open behind a server, he peeked inside. He was expecting to see a bunch of burnt out Baraboo kids back there, but instead it was a slick squad of Mexican dudes working in chaotic harmony. Looked like the back of any taco restaurant in Chicago.

The next day, Chris put the finishing touches on his love letter and then packed his bag for Chicago. He emailed Rob the final draft, thinking he might need the whole weekend, but within an hour he had a Spanish copy back in his inbox. What efficiency! Mr. Montoya must be more skilled than he was letting on. Once Chris was all packed, his mom and dad dropped him off at the Wisconsin Dells fast-food-nightmare parking lot. One big hug for each when the bus arrived, then he boarded the bus, settled into his seat, and dozed off as the bus rambled down the highway back to Chicago.

When school resumed on Monday, everyone was hustling and bustling to get to the finish line. Lessons were changed, then un-changed, then re-changed to death, and every day the students got more and more eager for summer to arrive. Chris's classes were grooving, behavior was great and engagement was sufficient. Even Javy was keeping it together. He was working hard, goofy enough in class to be funny, but not enough to be a major distraction, and stopping by once or twice a week to make sure he got all the material.

Every day he could, Chris grabbed the translated letter from his desk and went out front to see if he could catch Jaslene alone. He had asked Javy to have him text him a few times so he could tell her how great Javy was doing, but she never reached out. In fact, when he thought about it, he hadn't heard from her since before Spring Break. All the more reason to ask her out as soon as possible. But each day he was out front, something delayed the move. One day she was talking with a few other moms, another her and Javy sped off before he had the chance, and then one week she must have been working late because Javy got a ride with another mom.

April turned to May and Chris started to worry. He didn't want Jaslene to forget what they had, the chats they shared, the connection they built. He had to ask her out soon. The next Tuesday, the stars aligned and he got his chance.

It was a beautiful afternoon; the sun was shining, the birds were chirping, and the kids were screeching. Chris saw Jaslene waiting alone by her car, looking as beautiful as ever in her dark blue scrubs, and he knew this was his shot. He clutched the translation in his hand and walked over to her car.

"Jaslene, hello!"

"Oh, hi."

Chris stopped two feet away, took two deep breaths, and began. "Jaslene. Creo que eres tan hermosa como una rosa y dulce como aguas frescas–"

From the school's front door, Chris heard a piercing scream. He turned and saw Javy sprinting towards them. "NOOOOOOOOOOOOOO!!!" He yelled as he ran. What was Javy doing? Was he mad that Chris was asking out his mom? How could he know his intentions? It didn't matter, either way, he had to finish quick.

"Cada vez que te enviamos mensajes de texto," Chris looked back and Javy was about twenty yards away. He turned back to Jaslene, "Mi cariño por ti se hace más y más–"

Chris thought he was doing great, his pronunciation was just like he practiced with the videos online, but then he looked up and Jaslene looked confused. She interrupted him, "Excuse me, what is going on?"

Chris paused. She didn't even have an accent. "What?" He stammered.

"What are you talking about?"

"Wait, you can speak–"

Javy was running so fast that when he got to Jaslene and Chris, he didn't have room to stop and slammed into the car, dropping to the ground like a loose skeleton. Chris and Jaslene both gasped, but Javy bounced right back up and jammed himself in between them. He put two hands on Chris's stomach and started trying to push him backwards.

"Mr. Krause, NOOO DOOOOOOON'T!!!"

"Javy, what are you doing?" Jaslene spat.

"Jaslene, your English?"

"What about it?"

"But you said, I mean, when you texted you said…"

"When have I ever texted you?"

Having heard Javy's collision with the car, Principal Roth-Ramirez hustled over to see what the commotion was, and arrived just in time to see Javy give up trying to push Chris and lay down on the ground with his hands covering his face.

"Mr. Krause, Ms. Garcia, is everything okay over here? Is Javy okay?"

Jaslene nudged Javy with her foot. "Javy, are you okay?" He nodded from his horizontal state. "He's fine, he runs into things all the time. But Javy's math teacher, excuse me, what was your name again?"

Chris was too flustered to speak. Principal Roth-Ramirez answered for him, "This is Mr. Krause."

"So I don't know if you have me confused for someone else or what, but Mr. Krause was trying to read me, like, a love letter or something? I don't know, but in Spanish? I don't think it's really appropriate to be honest, I'm just trying to pick up Javy and go home."

Principal Roth-Ramirez turned to Chris, "Mr. Krause, what were you reading her?" Chris tried to answer, but no words came out.

She saw the letter in his hand and motioned for Chris to give it to her. When he didn't move, Principal Roth-Ramirez pulled it out of his hands and started to read.

"Mr. Krause, why were you reading Ms. Garcia a love letter in Spanish?" Before he could answer, they were joined by Ms. Weyman, the Assistant Principal.

"Principal Roth-Ramirez, everything okay here?"

"We might have a bit of a situation actually. Is Mr. Diaz in today?"

"He's not, he's downtown."

"Can you get Mr. Bishop, I think we need the Title IX coordinator here."

"I'm on it."

"Matter of fact, get the Union Rep too. That's Ms. Romero, right?"

"Correct."

"Great, can you bring them here please."

"On it."

Principal Roth-Ramirez pointed at Chris. "You stay here." Then she looked back at Jaslene. "Ms. Garcia, I am extremely sorry about this. We'll get this sorted out right away."

Jaslene crossed her arms and rolled her eyes. Chris could feel his hands moisten with sweat. He looked back to the school and saw Rob and a few other young teachers looking at them and snickering. Javy was curled up into the fetal position and slowly yanking out handfuls of grass and piling them on top of his head and body. Chris wished he could do the same. They stood in silence for an excruciating three minutes. Eventually, Ms. Weyman arrived with Mr. Bishop and Ms. Romero in tow.

Principal Roth-Ramirez addressed the group. "Okay, so, Ms. Garcia if I may." Jaslene nodded. "Ms. Garcia was waiting to pick up her son Javy, who is in Mr. Krause's math class, and Mr. Krause walked over and started reading her this letter. From what I understand, they have not spoken in person or otherwise prior to today.

Is that correct Ms. Garcia?" Jaslene nodded again. Principal Roth-Ramirez handed the letter to the others. They inspected it closely. "Mr. Krause, would you care to explain why you decided to read a love letter written in Spanish to Ms. Garcia this afternoon?"

All Chris could do was sputter, "The texts, we texted. The texts." He took his phone out of his pocket and fumbled to his inbox. He clicked on his text thread with Jaslene and handed his phone to Principal Roth-Ramirez. She read and scrolled and read and scrolled, then handed the phone to Ms. Weyman who read the texts while Mr. Bishop and Ms. Romero looked over her shoulder.

"Ms. Garcia, is this your phone number?" Ms. Weyman held out the phone to Jaslene. She squinted at the screen.

"Yes it is…but I never sent those texts. I don't even have Mr. Krause's phone number."

"Can we see your phone?"

"Sure."

Jaslene handed her phone to Ms. Weyman. Holding both phones, she pressed the call icon on Chris's screen and Jaslene's phone lit up with a call from *Coll y Cuchí Main Office*.

"Why is his number saved in your phone as our main office?"

"What? I have no idea. I didn't even, I mean, I never saved that."

"Does anyone else ever use your phone?"

"Only…"

They all turned and looked down at Javy, who was still lying on the ground, covered with blades of grass. He peeked out from behind his hands and saw the six adults looking his way, then he groaned, slowly rolled over, and began burrowing his face into the schoolyard dirt.

— — —

Two months later, Javy sat in the passenger seat of his mom's sedan as they drove into the parking lot of a low-slung strip mall in

Garfield Park. Jaslene pulled to the curb in front of a pushed-back door that read *Wellness Insight* in curly green script. She turned to Javy.

"You want me to go in with you?"

"No, no. I'm fine. I can go in alone."

"I'll be waiting here in the lot when you finish. Call me if you don't see me."

"Okay."

"Be good."

"I will."

Jaslene leaned over and kissed his head. "Love you, baby."

"Love you too."

Javy got out of the car and softly shut the door behind him. He took two steps towards Wellness Insight and looked back. His mom was still sitting at the curb, watching him walk in. He gave her a look, she shrugged. He flicked his wrist twice, she rolled her eyes then drove off to find a parking spot.

As he got to the door, it flew open from the inside. Javy jumped back just in time.

"Yo, watch out." He said.

"Sorry. Excuse me."

Javy looked up at the man's face.

"Mr. Krause?!" Mr. Krause's eyes bugged out for a second, then rebooted quickly.

"Javy. Hi."

"What are you doing here, Mr. Krause?"

"I umm, well, umm…"

"You got therapy too, huh?"

Mr. Krause laughed. "Yeah, yeah I do."

"Principal Roth-Ramirez make you go?"

"The union mostly."

"I feel that brother, my mom signed me up. Who you talking to?"

"Dr. Berkson."

"No way! Me too. How is he?"

"Good, today was good. It was my first session."

"We must be twins, Mr. Krause."

"Guess we must be." Javy felt the soft breeze against his arms. "Well, I have to run. Good seeing you, Javy."

"You too, Mr. Krause."

Mr. Krause gave him a pat on the shoulder, and as he turned away, Javy looked and saw his mom pulling the car into the parking spot closest to the door. She flicked her wrist at him twice and pointed at her watch, Javy nodded back. He stepped inside and watched from behind the glass door as Mr. Krause walked out of the parking lot and crossed the street.

Rums

Write and Wrong Cocktail Lounge Specials

Fahrenheit-151

2 oz Bacardi 151

1 oz coconut rum

3 oz pineapple juice

Ice cubes

Garnish with a lit match

Serve without books

Tart of Darkness

1 oz dark spiced rum

1 oz palm wine

3 oz Cream de Cassis

1/2 teaspoon activated charcoal

1 oz blackberry juice

1 oz lemon juice

Garnish with two black cherries

Serve in an imitation-ivory glass

The Rum Also Rises

1 oz dark rum

1 oz light rum

4 oz Red Bull

Garnish with a sprig of oregano and a lemon slice

Serve inscrutable

Molasses Shrugged

2 oz dark rum

1 oz molasses

2 oz ginger ale

2 shakes of cinnamon

Garnish with a cinnamon stick

Bring ingredients to the patron and let them make the drink their own damn self

A Confederacy of Punches

1 oz light rum

1 oz dark rum

0.5 oz grenadine

4 oz punch mix

Punch mix 1: 1/2 orange juice, 1/2 pineapple juice

Punch mix 2: 3/4 grapefruit juice, 1/4 lime juice

Punch mix 3: 1/2 cranberry juice, 1/2 strawberry lemonade

Garnish with slices of orange, lime, and lemon (respectively)

Coat the glass rim with Kool-Aid powder

Serve three at a time

4

For Reverent Green

At the edge of a glen, under the bluff and near the river, there was a tree. The tree enjoyed the crisp air on his trunk, the breeze ruffling his leaves, and the birds that would nest in his branches and chirp-chirp all day long. One day, he felt an odd sensation. A rhythmic pounding at the bottom of his trunk. It felt like he was being ripped apart. The *thwacks* vibrated up his body to his branches and leaves, until he felt a snap, then the air felt less crisp and the breeze disappeared and the birds flew away. He began to tilt over and everything went black.

When he woke up, his senses were askew. He looked down and saw he had four legs. He looked up and realized he could move his head. He looked around and realized he had eyes. Sunlight had the same warmth, but it no longer made him full like it used to. He touched his paws to another tree, it was hard and rough. He dug his snout into the ground and smelled the earth, it was sharp and sour. He licked the dirt, it tasted fine. He had turned into a dog.

The tree looked back at where he once stood, and all that was left was his stump and roots. His body had been taken. Walking up to his stump, he inhaled deeply, and could smell seasons past. The years of drought where his branches dried up and fell off, the years of plenty where his leaves were so lush that the grass below begged him to let light through. He stuck his nose in the air and followed the smell of himself towards the river.

When he got to the river, the scent grew thin. He shuffled to and fro, trying to latch back on, but the rush of the river must have washed it away. He searched around for any part of him, a branch or some bark or even a leaf, but everything he found was from someone else. In the distance, he saw a turtle sitting on the bank of the river, watching him. He walked over.

"Mr. Turtle! Mr. Turtle! Have you seen my body?" The turtle gazed up at him.

"I believe I am looking at it right now."

"No, not this body. My trunk and my branches."

"As a turtle, I am loath to say this, but you must slow down."

"What?"

"You are a dog."

"I am a tree."

"But you are a dog."

"Yes, yes, I *look* like a dog, but I've always been a tree, and I am looking for my body so that I can return to being a tree."

"Of course, I used to be that rock over there, but now I am a turtle."

"Really?!"

"No."

"Which rock were you?"

"Is your brain in your dog head or with your tree body?"

"You are very confusing, Mr. Turtle."

"Perhaps it would be better if I were a rock."

"But you have such a beautiful shell!"

"We have lost ourselves, how can I help you?"

"I am looking for myself."

"I can see that."

"Have you seen a tree with a thick trunk and many branches that was not attached to its stump?"

"Hmm. This morning a human brought many pieces of wood to this river and floated them downstream."

"Was it wood of my body?!"

"I most certainly do not know, but if you follow the river, you may find out."

"Thank you! Thank you Mr. Turtle! I will not forget you and your rock friends when I return."

The tree turned and began to run along the river, following its twists and turns, smelling all the while. Soon, he found his scent on the bank of the river. Its trail took him into the woods, through a narrow clearing, and onto a path that split into two branches. He paused at the fork. His scent was on both paths, and he didn't know which one to follow. He looked around to see if he could find any more clues, and high above him, sitting in the tree at the point of the fork, was a dark owl. He walked over to the tree.

"Ms. Owl! Ms. Owl!"

"Who?"

"You Ms. Owl! Can you help me?"

"Who?"

"Ms. Owl, please."

"I'm sorry, sometimes I cannot resist."

"Can you help me? I was a tree, but now I am a dog, and I am looking for myself." The owl shrugged. "Have you seen a man with many pieces of wood? I think this is the man that took my body."

"I see everything in this forest. A sparrow cannot leave its nest without my notice."

"Did you see a man come from the river?"

"A mouse cannot visit their aunt or uncle in the dark of night without me seeing their every move."

"A man? Was there a man?"

"Even a lily beetle cannot take a date to dinner at a maple leaf without me knowing their reservation time."

"This man would have been quite a bit bigger than a lily beetle."

"Humans typically are."

"*If* a man were to have passed with my body, you would have seen him?"

"Without a doubt."

"So, did you?"

"Did I, what?"

"Did you see today a man pass with a tree in tow?"

"Down which path?"

"That's what I'm asking Ms. Owl?"

"Who?"

"The man with the wood!"

"It's a solitary life for an old Owl like myself. My mate has long passed, my children have all left the nest to find their own mates further up the river, and they say they will come to see me, but they don't visit very often."

"Who?"

"My children. There's Ariel, my oldest. Then Barney, my second. Hootie is my youngest son. I was worried about him for many years after he fell in with a rough crowd of woodpeckers, but he got his life back together and just found a lovely mate–"

"Who?"

"Her name is Ava and her family actually comes from down south–"

"Who?"

"Ava, my son's mate."

"Ms. Owl."

"Yes?"

"The man."

"Who?"

"The man with the wood!"

"Oh yes, he came by this morning when the sun was still new in the sky. He had a big pile of wood on his cart and it took up the north branch of the path. He does not live far, just a few minutes up the path."

"Thank you Ms. Owl!"

The tree took off in a sprint down the path, and as the wind rushed into his face, he could smell his scent growing stronger and stronger. He was close. Suddenly, a loud *thwack* stopped him in his tracks. The same *thwack* he felt this morning, he could now hear echoing through the air. He approached slowly and saw the man toss some pieces of wood into a pile then walk back to a log with an ax. The log was part of him, the tree could feel it.

As the man raised his ax to strike, the tree ran over and barked at him to stop.

"Sir! Sir! You must stop! That is my body!" The man began to yell back, but he could not articulate himself and his words were unintelligible.

"Arg-er-arg hur-gur-gur! Bargarbargarbar-gar!"

"You have no right! Put down your ax!"

"Aar gar! Raga-raga-raga-rurr!"

Talking would be pointless, the man could not be reached. He flashed his teeth and the man froze. The tree tried to grab the log with his paws, but it was stuck and he could not move it. He tried to bite into the log and push with his legs, but the log stayed put. The man ran over and began to swing at him with the ax, but the tree was able to dodge the tool and run around the man to the big pile of wood. The man followed him over, and when he got close, the tree lunged at the man's ankles. The man tried to jump back, but his feet slipped, and his body fell forward, and he hit the ground with a tremendous *thud*. The tree grabbed the biggest branch he could find in between his teeth and ran towards the man. He tried to roll out of the way, but he could not get far enough, and the branch smacked him across his head. The man rolled onto his back and let out a long groan.

The tree gripped the branch tight in his teeth and bolted back down the path. When he got to the fork he shouted out through the side of his mouth, "Ms. Owl! Ms. Owl! I've found myself!"

The owl looked down at him and said, "Sometimes you don't know what you've found until it finds you."

"No, I know what this is. It's me!

The tree continued running through the forest, to the river, where he turned upstream and cut back into the clearing. He saw the turtle and shouted out, "Mr. Turtle! Mr. Turtle! I've found myself!"

The turtle looked up at him and said, "That is a branch."

The tree ran and ran and ran until he arrived back at his roots. He gently placed the branch on top of his stump and took a step back to admire his work. The sun shined brighter, the birds chirped louder, and the air smelled more fresh now that one of his branches was back in its rightful place. Then, he turned around and ran back towards the river to get back more of himself.

Whiskys

Write and Wrong Cocktail Lounge Specials

The Catcher in the Rye

3 oz rye whisky

½ teaspoon of cold water

3 dashes imitation Peychaud's bitters

2 dashes imitation Angostura bitters

1 cube of Splenda (or other sugar substitute)

Imitation Absinthe to rinse

Garnish with a plastic lemon peel

Serve self-righteously

The Rye Who Came in From the Cold

2 oz rye whiskey

2.5 oz Bailey's Irish Cream

1.5 oz coffee liqueur

A dash of heavy cream

Ice cubes

Serve deceptively

Barley & Me
2 oz barleywine
1 oz Scotch whisky
7 oz light beer
Garnish with a stalk of barley
Serve carefully

Extremely Loud and Incredibly Alcoholic
2 oz rye whiskey
2 oz bourbon whiskey
2 oz scotch whiskey
1 oz sweet vermouth
2 dashes Angostura bitters
1 dash orange bitters
Garnish with a lemon twist
Serve slammed down onto the table

5

Lyndell Rides the Train

I knew Lyndell was up to something when he didn't do his sleep checks. We shared a room back then, and Lyndell said that since I was the younger brother, I wasn't allowed to fall asleep before he did. So every night, after Mom and Dad sent us to bed and we got all nice and tucked in, Lyndell would call out *Sleep Check!* from his side of the room, and I would have to confirm that I was still awake. If I didn't answer, he would call out again and again, and if I still didn't answer, he would start tossing his ratty tennis shoes at me until I woke up. Then five minutes later, he'd call out another sleep check, and so on and so on till he fell asleep. Most nights, Lyndell would nod off after two or three sleep checks, but some nights he would toss and turn for hours. I made sure to always keep a book by my bedside, both to keep myself occupied for when Lyndell couldn't sleep and to bat away any incoming projectiles for when I couldn't stay awake.

Before we moved to Uptown, Lyndell never saw it fit to demand my consciousness, but once we got settled in the new apartment on Margate Terrace, he decided to expand his prerogative as the older brother. We moved right after my Bar Mitzvah, and our new apartment was one swell nest. Each unit came equipped with its own rotary dial telephone, a big upgrade from the pay phone in the hallway closet we had to use back on the West Side. Brand new dishwasher, a fold-out ironing board in the kitchen…there was even a special outlet hook-up for televisions in the living room! Of course, Mom and Dad, stubborn as all hell, told us not to even *look* at the outlet. They didn't have TVs when they were growing up, so they didn't see why we needed one. They said we were lucky to be able to turn on a radio dial and hear Nat King Cole or Sammy Kaye whenever we pleased. Funny how they sprung for a TV right after Lyndell and I moved out. But anyway.

It was the Saturday right after Thanksgiving, basketball season was starting the next week, and Lyndell would not stop talking about how good their team at Siegel High School was going to be this year. Dribble-drive this and set-shot that, day in and day out. When he wasn't down at the courts practicing, Lyndell and his friend Abe were hanging around the kitchen and giggling like a pair of schoolgirls. I saw them standing in the doorway, drawing on popsicle sticks over each other's heads the past few mornings. They were doing it again on Friday night before Mom sent Abe packing. I thought that maybe they were doing a school project. Guess it was in a way.

That Saturday night, Lyndell got ready for bed in a hurry. He brushed his teeth and was in bed before I could even kick off my slippers. As always, I turned off the lights and fumbled my way into bed, then waited for the sleep checks to come. But that night, no checks arrived. Three, four, five minutes passed and Lyndell was as quiet as a mouse. Now sometimes Lyndell would fall asleep fast, but never that fast. He always got at least one or two sleep checks in, if anything just to make sure I knew he didn't forget about them. I looked over and his eyes were wide open, he was just lying there staring at the ceiling. I read my book for another few minutes, then looked back over, and now that my eyes had adjusted to the dark, I noticed that he was wearing a collared shirt under the covers. Something didn't add up.

I leaned over and whispered, "Hey Lyndell, you up?"

Nothing.

A bit louder, "Are you asleep already?"

Still nothing.

"Lyndell, I can see your eyes. I know you're not asleep."

He shut his eyes tight and slowed his breathing.

"You can't fool me, I know you're awake."

Lyndell kept his eyes closed and hissed back, "Shut up Siggy. Go to sleep."

"Why are you wearing a collared shirt to bed?"

"None of your business."

"Planning on dreaming about a hot date?"

"Shut up!"

"Make me."

"Don't make me make you."

"Make me make me, buttermilk cake me." Then I started doing this low croaking noise with my throat that Lyndell hated, and that finally got to him.

"Fine! Fine! But you have to promise not to tell Mom and Dad."

"I plomise."

"I'm serious!"

"Okay, okay, I promise."

"Follow me."

Lyndell got out from under his covers. Not only did he have a collared shirt on, but he had on slack and socks to boot! He held one finger in front of his mouth and shushed me as I put down my book and got out of bed. He opened our bedroom door real slow, then we tip-toed past Mom and Dad's room and into the living room. He slipped on his shoes and opened the side door to the fire escape. He motioned me outside with him.

Down below in the alley, Abe was leaning up against the wall, spinning a pen around in his hand.

"Abe and I got plans tonight." Lyndell glared at me. "There. You happy?"

"You're sneaking out?"

"No! We're just…going out for a bit."

"Where are you going?"

"Nowhere, we're gonna to go ride the train."

"Ride the train? Sounds boring." Lyndell rolled his eyes. "So boring in fact..." I took a step back inside and Lyndell grabbed my shoulder, pulling me back out. He told me their plan.

Turns out, Lyndell and Abe weren't going out to get somewhere. They were going out to get shorter. See, back in those days, schools didn't have Varsity and Junior Varsity and Freshman B-Squad and all that. They had two teams: Bigs and Littles. Didn't matter your age, didn't matter your skills; if you were five-foot-eight or taller, you played in the Bigs, and if you were shorter than five-foot-eight, you played in the Littles. In the morning, everyone on the North Side would go to Torrio Technical High School to get their measurements and Lyndell and Abe were hoping to be the biggest Littles in the city.

Last year when they were Juniors at Siegel High, Lyndell and Abe were on the Littles and led their team to an undefeated regular season. They were primed to sweep the playoffs as well, but in the City Championship, they lost to Saint Alphonse's Academy in a knock-down, drag-em-out, slugfest of a game. Lyndell sulked around the house for weeks after, and ever since, he had not stopped training with Abe to come back this season and, as he would say, shove the basketball so far down Saint Al's throat that they would be shitting orange. But now that the season was about to start, they had one problem. They grew.

Lyndell had been trying to think of ways to rig the measure-in, see if maybe he could bring his own yardstick or find some pants he could hide his bent legs in. Luckily, before he tried anything stupid, science came to the rescue. His biology teacher told the class one day that due to the evolution of our bodies, gravity compresses our spines while we're standing up and we all shrink during the day, only to grow back at night when we sleep. Lyndell became convinced that gravity was his path back to the Littles. Him and Abe measured themselves first thing in the morning and last thing at night, and the record reflected that Abe shrunk from five-nine and a quarter to five-eight and a half over the course of one day. Lyndell went from five-eight and three-quarters to five-eight and one-quarter. They figured if they stayed out all night before the measure-in, they would each lose another half-inch at least, and then be able to take their revenge on the Littles of Saint Alphonse's.

Their plan was to ride the train back and forth for a while, then get off downtown and see if there was a theater they could sneak into for a show. From there, they would make their way north to Torrio Tech, be there when the doors opened, then get measured and get back home before Mom and Dad even woke up. Sounded like fun.

I put my hands on my hips, "I'm coming with."

"Like hell you are."

"If you can stay up all night, then so can I."

"Siggy, you promised…"

"Yeah, I promised that I wouldn't tell Mom and Dad. But if I have to go back inside, the bedroom might get all spooky with me being alone and I might have to go knock on Mom and Dad's door and then who knows…"

Lyndell twisted his face and spat against the wall. "Let me talk to Abe. Don't move."

I watched as Lyndell walked down the steps and over to Abe. They slapped hands and I could tell Abe was asking what the deal was, but I couldn't hear what they were saying. Some of Lyndell's friends might have been mad at my attempted intrusion, but Abe always treated me like an equal. If I had a shot with anyone, it was him. They had a few words back and forth, then seemed to come to a consensus. Lyndell waved me down and I met him at the bottom of the fire escape.

"Okay, you can come with. But you gotta stay awake the whole night. We're not gonna carry you around the city like some baby. And no sitting down either, if we stand, you stand. Got it?"

"Yes sir! I'll be back in two minutes flat."

I ran back inside and changed as quickly and quietly as I could. I closed the fire escape door with a hushed click, then hurried down the stairs and skipped over to Lyndell and Abe.

Abe smiled, "What took you so long, Sig?"

"Sorry, I had to find my gallivanting shoes!" Abe laughed and Lyndell smacked me upside my head. I rubbed the spot of contact, "So, where to first fellas?"

———

At my request, we made a quick visit to the corner store for some potato chips before we got on the train. They just started selling these chips with sharp ridges that crunched like crazy when you bit into them. Lyndell and Abe stayed outside while I browsed, but then I realized I didn't have any money on me, so I dragged Lyndell inside and made him give me a dime to get my chips. He grumbled the rest of the way to the train, but once we got to the platform, his spirits were lifted by the clamor of the crowd. Friday night on the Howard line, it was hopping. All the prim and proper citizens would be heading north at this hour, we were riding south with the more irregular elements of the city. There were some Army men sitting up front, probably riding downtown to meet with some respectable young women for a respectable evening. There was a crusty group of beatniks in the corner, instruments in tow, heading down to the Jazz clubs looking for a musical fix. Then us. Just three young men, standing by the door, trying to shrink.

Lyndell and Abe rapped about school and cracked jokes about names I didn't know, I hung close and tried to be slick while gawking at our trainmates. At the Fullerton stop, the door opened and a kid wearing a sharp three-piece suit walked on board. Abe stopped mid-sentence and looked over.

Lyndell gave Abe an elbow to the side, "You like the cut of his jib?"

Abe elbowed him back, "I think I met him." He called over, "Hey! Frank?"

The suit turned around, "Yes?" He tapped his finger on his chin three times then pointed it back at Abe. "Mr…"

"Bachman, Abe Bachman."

"Of course, of course. Did we meet at one of those college fairs?"

"Yes! Siegel High School."

"Spectacular." Our new friend stepped into our circle. "Great to see you again Abe." Then he turned to Lyndell and extended his arm. "Franklin Deleno Rosenson, you can call me Frank. Nice to meet you."

I could see Lyndell gripping hard as he shook Frank's hand. "Lyndell Silverstein. This here is my little brother Siggy."

I shot my hand out and grabbed Frank's, shaking it hard just like Lyndell. "I'm Siggy." I said to him, putting a little extra chest into my voice.

Frank smiled. "Nice to meet you too, young fella."

"I'm not that young, I'm in high school."

"My apologies, I should have known."

Abe butted back in, "You're looking sharp tonight Frank! where are you headed?"

"I'm going to the University Club. The Chicago Bar Association is having an event and I got invited to stop by for the reception after dinner."

Abe's eyes opened wide, "That's so cool. At the fair you said you were in law school, right?"

Frank laughed, "I wish. I'm pre-law, up at University of Wisconsin. Just started my second year."

Lyndell sucked his teeth. "Franklin. Deleno. Rosenson. That's some name."

Frank laughed again, "Yeah, yeah, I get that a lot. Easy to remember at least."

Abe laughed. Lyndell didn't.

"How'd your parents settle on that?" Lyndell asked.

"Well, my mom had me real soon after she and my dad moved to the states, and everyone told them how well the Jews were doing for ourselves here in America, so they wanted to name me after the most successful Jewish American they could find."

"I didn't know Franklin Roosevelt was Jewish!" I yelped.

"No, well, he wasn't. But my mom worked as a maid at this house up in Kenilworth, and they would always complain about FDR and his *Jew Deal*, so she thought he must have been one of us. Guess no one told her otherwise."

Abe laughed hard, "That's one hell of a story Frank, one hell of story. Say, how do you like it up at Wisconsin? I'm working on applying to schools right now and I'm real interested in studying law too…"

While Frank and Abe kept talking, Lyndell started to get bored of the conversation. He made no attempt to hide it and eventually wandered off to the other side of the train. I hung around and listened for a while. Frank told Abe all about his classes at Wisconsin and what he heard about other schools. Abe knew a ton about all the different colleges and programs, I had never realized how complicated the decisions could be. Lyndell never talked about colleges at all. Every few weeks, Dad would come into our room and throw an application for the City Colleges at Lyndell, and every time, Lyndell would stuff them in his backpack and go back to whatever else he was doing.

Once we got to the Loop, Frank shook Abe's hand then reached down to shake mine before stepping off and shuffling down the platform. Once the doors closed, Lyndell walked back over and scowled at Abe.

"You thinking of skipping town on me next year?"

"Just keeping my options open, Lyndell."

"Let's switch trains."

At the next stop, we transferred to the Jackson Park line and headed south.

— — —

In the next train car, I wandered around a bit and found a spot on a grab rail next to a young couple. More passengers got on at the next few stops and I ended up pressed so close to them that I couldn't help but eavesdrop. It sounded like they were coming back from a night downtown and the woman was razzing the man for wearing an old Zoot Suit. It had too much fabric, but it was also cut to his body at strange intervals, so he ended up looking like a Renaissance prince going through a Jump Jazz phase. They went back and forth arguing about whether the people at Italian Village were pointing at them out of respect or derision. The woman fiddled with the zipper of her purse and I could see the seams of her gloves starting to fray. After I got bored of their squabbling, I squeezed my way over to where Lyndell and Abe were standing.

Lyndell put his arm around my shoulder, "I was wondering where you went. Don't get lost now."

"I won't, I won't."

We rode in silence for a minute or two, then Lyndell patted my head. "Say, did I ever tell you about the first official basketball game that Abe and I ever played together?"

I had heard the story a million times, but I could see that Lyndell wanted to tell it again, so I nodded my head no and off he went.

Abe and Lydell had been best friends since they both went to the same Kindergarten back in Lawndale. They were attached at the hip at school, and Lydell even convinced Dad to let him go to synagogue with Abe's family. No small feat since they went to Beit Begadim, the laundryman's shul on Avers – which just so happened to be the bitter rival of our shul, Beit Beged Yam, the landryman's shul on Ridgeway. My father figured it was a chore to get him to the synagogue in the first place, better Beit Begadim than a whorehouse he would say. I always thought he was a little harsh on the women of Beit Ayroom, but that's neither here nor there.

Lyndell had been obsessed with basketball since he was old enough to dribble a ball, but Abe had barely shot a single hoop till they went off to middle school. It took Lyndell all his might to convince Abe to join the team at Lansky Secondary, but convince him he did, and his love of the game slowly spread to Abe like a tired influenza. Their coach was a gym teacher who had been hired through the West Side Democratic Party's patronage program, so at practice he would just roll out the balls and sit in the corner smoking a cigar while Lyndell would lead the team in drills and exercises.

Their first game was against Colosimo Middle School in Little Italy. Lyndell was talking the whole week before about how sweet it was going to be to show them who ran the West Side. They drilled hard to prepare, but Colosimo was a scrappy bunch, and neither team could figure out how to get their jump shots to go in. The coach wasn't much help in the huddles, he had spent most of the first half reading a newspaper and at halftime when Lyndell asked what he saw on the court, the only thing he said was that the other team looked seedy.

The second half was back and forth, or as back and forth as a game with under thirty total points scored could be. No team could pull ahead, and with twelve seconds left in the fourth quarter, Colosimo had the ball up by one point. Lyndell pressed up on their point guard and shouted for a trap, but when he looked for Abe, he was, as Lyndell put it, standing around with one thumb in his mouth and the other thumb plum up his ass. Seeing no other option, Lyndell dove for the ball and ended up knocking both him and the Colosimo player to the ground. The ball bounced right to Abe, who stood there frozen in fear, until the entire team yelled at him to run. He took off dribbling towards their basket, nothing but open space ahead of him.

In practice, Abe always had this bad habit of coming at layups straight away. Lyndell would hector him to go at it from an angle so he could use the backboard, but for whatever reason, Abe couldn't shake the middle. So on that day, as Abe barreled down the court, Lyndell yelled out, *The side! The side!* and wouldn't you know it, Abe somehow found himself at the perfect angle. But he was going fast. Too fast. By the time he released the ball, he was directly under the basket. His shot ricocheted off the bottom of the rim and donked him right in his face, knocking him down to the ground. He lay there like a dead fish as the ball rolled out of bounds and the buzzer sounded, ending the game.

"He was on the ground for five whole minutes before we could get him to stand up!" Lyndell laughed.

Abe scowled, "It wasn't five minutes."

"Was too. And his face was as red as a pizza pie when he finally did."

"That doesn't even make sense, pizzas aren't all red."

Lyndell pinched his fingers together and shook them back and forth, "Just like a-Mama Bertucci's a-famous pizza-pie."

As the train kept rumbling south, my legs started getting a bit weary. Lydell was still sassing Abe, so I wandered off and found an empty seat. I pressed my head up against the window and watched the lights of downtown fade into the distance. My eyelids started to get a little heavy, so I closed them for just a second to rest, but I must have dozed off because next thing I knew, I felt Lyndell's knuckles jabbing me in the ribs and opened my eyes just in time to see him real close, yelling *Sleep check!* right in my face.

Lyndell stood back and hung with both hands on the grab rail, looking real pleased with his work.

"No sleeping Siggy-baby. You wanted to come with, you gotta stay up just like us."

"Okay, okay." I wiped my eyes. "Where are we?"

Lyndell looked outside. "Well, we just passed the Stockyard Split–"

"Two stops ago," Abe added.

"–Two stops ago," Lyndell continued, "which means we are…"

Abe rolled his eyes, "Between 43rd and–"

"Dammit Abe, I knew that. Quit stepping on my toes while I'm trying to harangue my little brother here." Abe put both hands in the air and waddled backwards. "We're around 45th Street, still heading south."

I turned around and looked out the window. "How far south are we going?"

"Jackson Park, then we'll ride back north. Now get on your feet soldier, pronto!"

I stood and gave my arms and legs a stretch. As I was bending down, the train started to screech against the tracks and we slowed to a crawl. I almost fell over, but Lyndell caught me before I fell and stood me back up straight. Everyone on the train looked around confused. As the train pulled into the 47th Street station, the intercom started buzzing, and when we came to a stop the doors opened, then closed, then opened again and stayed that way. Lyndell looked over at Abe who looked back with a shrug.

A voice crackled over the intercom, "Ladies and Gentlemen, sorry for the inconvenience, but this train is no longer in service. Please exit the train and platform. I repeat, this train is no longer in service, please exit the train and platform." Then the intercom clicked off and we were left with nothing but questions.

Lyndell went over to Abe and they conferred for a few seconds. He looked back over at me, "Siggy, come on, we're gonna go check with the conductor."

I followed Lyndell and Abe out the door. We marched up the platform to the front car and the conductor stepped out of his cab right as we arrived. He was dressed in black coveralls and a dirty White Sox cap. I wondered if they only give the blue and white striped ones to the conductors of the big trains.

Lyndell stopped short and called out to him, "Hey mister! What's going on with the train?"

The conductor took off his gloves and spit onto the tracks. "Track's broke kid. Needs repair."

I started to ask, "But what–"

Lyndell pushed me back, "Shut it, Siggy." He turned back to the conductor, "So when's this train going to run again?"

"We gotta check the train, check the tracks. The brakes might have got bent."

"So?"

"Sew buttons on your underwear, kid. Track's broke. No trains here till it's fixed."

The conductor walked past us to the track cottage on the edge of the platform and slammed the door shut.

Lyndell kicked the ground. "Shit. Shit shit shit."

Abe piped up, "Lyndell, maybe we should just call a cab. I bet they have a phone down in the station we could use."

"I look like I have cab fare?"

Abe dug into his pocket, "I brought a few dollars, maybe–"

"Put that away. We meant to stay out the night, right? It's barely eleven o'clock, let's walk."

"Walk where?"

"North. To Torrio."

Abe worried his watch with his right hand. "I dunno, I dunno Lyndell. Maybe we should just wait here. The train will start back eventually."

Lyndell glared back at him, "You want to stay here on this platform? We'll be bored to death!"

Abe looked around, "They usually have a timetable on the platforms somewhere."

Lyndell groaned, "How is the train going to run on schedule when the track's broken? Can't always plan for the next train Abe, sometimes you've got to make your own way."

"It's just–"

"What, are you scared?"

"I'm not scared!"

"Are you scared of," Lyndell leaned towards Abe and whispered, "*Black people?*"

"I'm not! You know I'm not!"

"Because we're in Bronzeville, and I don't know if you know this, but a lot of the people who live here are," Lyndell leaned in to whisper again, "*Black.*"

"Quit it! That ain't it and you know it."

"I don't know what I know, now do I?"

"What if we get lost or something?"

"You jamoke, how are we gonna get lost when I know this city like the back of my hand?"

"I'm just saying—"

"You think we're going to get robbed? Or kidnapped"

"No!"

"I'll admit, you're cute, but not as cute as that Lindbergh baby."

Abe hung his head, Lyndell had got to him. "I just, I just…"

Lyndell put his arm around Abe's shoulder and led him towards the platform stairs. "We'll be fine. Worst comes to worst, we can just find another train station and get back on there." I ran after, and when we got to the sidewalk exit, Lyndell pointed up at the street sign. "See, State Street. Just like downtown. We'll head north and find our way."

We were at State and 47th, Torrio Tech was at Addison and Western – three miles west and ten miles north. I looked up at the station clock right as it struck midnight.

— — —

Whenever Mom or Dad mentioned Bronzeville, they always talked all sideways about it. It was never clear whether they thought it was a place of refined culture or a place to be avoided at all costs. They would talk about the famous clubs and the restaurants with reverence, but it was clear they had never been and had no intention of ever going. Looking around as we walked up State Street, it didn't look much different than some parts of Uptown. Music wafting through the air, cars roaring down the street, and young couples strolling down the sidewalk. I tried to act as normal as possible. Me and my brother and Abe, walking down the street, like we've done hundreds of times. Normal, normal, normal. I had never had to try that hard to act normal before.

Lyndell must have noticed because he tousled my hair and gave me a warm smile, then he leaned over to Abe and said, "Say Abe, don't this remind you of our game Freshman year against McKee?"

"That was on the West Side."

"Shit, I'm not talking about geography."

I butted in, "Which game was that?"

Lyndell laughed, "You never pay attention do you Siggy?" He turned to Abe, "You want to fill him in?"

During Lyndell and Abe's freshman year, they both went to Morton High School on the West Side, where our families still lived. The neighborhood was changing. When I was born, it was still almost all Jewish, but by the time Lyndell got to High School, Black families had started to move in and there was tension bubbling up on the streets. McKee High School was a mile or so east of Morton, and had been a Black school for years. A lot of Black families were none too happy about the way they were all being crammed into McKee when there were open seats at Morton, and some of the Jewish families were none too happy about the Black families being none too happy. The basketball court was one of the few places the schools still met, and the game that season was a brawl. And that's not a metaphor.

The game was on McKee's home court and the gym seemed designed to make it feel like the crowd was going to come crashing down on you at any second. The gym floor only extended a few feet beyond the sidelines, and the brick walls that boxed in the floor were only around eight feet high. Seats for the fans pushed right to the edge, so they were pretty much looking right down on you when you were on the sidelines. It was no long distance for a kernel of popcorn or a malted milk ball or a loogie to travel.

Lyndell and Abe were the youngest players on the Littles team, they had yet to play a single minute that season. Their seats at the end of the bench gave them a perfect view to watch the game descend into pure chaos. From the jump, pushing and shoving gave way to elbows and fists and flagrant fouls. Insults were hurled and fights broke out every other possession. While scrambling for a loose ball, a necklace with a cross pendant was ripped from a McKee player's neck and thrown to the ground. That was quickly followed by a kippah being snatched from Yossol Levin's head and frisbee-tossed into the stands. Luckily our coach kept a few extra in his gym bag so Yossol was still kosher to play.

One by one, all the upperclassmen fouled out or got ejected, and by pure necessity, Lyndell and Abe both found themselves on the court in the fourth quarter. The crowd was relentless, cheering and yelling non-stop, hurling insults and booing with all their might. Lyndell quickly got into the spirit of the game when he and a McKee player got locked up going for a rebound. The referee, not wanting to get close enough to catch a stray fist, let them duke it out until the two coaches ran out onto the court and pulled the players back to their benches.

With ten seconds left in the game, McKee was up by one point and Morton's coach called a timeout to huddle them up. Lyndell and Abe listened closely for the last play, but instead, their coach started going over their post-game exit plan. Win or lose, he didn't want to risk spending one more second than necessary in that gym, so he told the team that one of the other coaches was pulling the bus around back as they spoke, and after that buzzer sounded, they were to run out the door under their basket to the parking lot and get on the bus as quickly as possible. Abe looked at their bench and his teammates were already packing up their bags and grabbing everything they could. The ref blew the whistle and Lyndell asked what the play was. Their coach shrugged and told them to improvise.

Abe inbounded the ball to Lyndell and he was met with a trap when he got near half-court. Lyndell floated a pass across the court, and one of the McKee players knocked it backwards, but Abe was able to grab it and sprint back up the court. He looked straight ahead and saw the door under the basket crack open and one of their coaches peek in. Then he looked up at the clock and saw five seconds left. Then he looked at the crowd and saw a mass of fans looking like they were ready to take a whole lot more than a basketball game's worth of anger out on anyone they could get their hands on, so he threw the ball up as high as he could in the general direction of the basket, and ran straight for the door. Before the ball even landed, he slipped outside and dove into the back door of the team bus. The buzzer sounded and the crowd exploded.

Not five seconds later, the rest of the Morton team burst through the door and started clamoring their way into the bus. As the team piled on, each player was increasingly covered in candy, soda, and all sorts of other unidentifiable gobs and goos. Lyndell was the last one in the gym, he was walking backwards, shouting at the fans who were grabbing at him, and their coach had to reach back through the door to pull him out. When he finally got on the bus, his jersey was ripped, his shorts were stained cola-brown, and an ice cream sundae sat upside-down on his head like a sailor's hat. The door slammed shut and the coach yelled *Go! Go! Go!*, and the bus lurched forward.

Everyone was quiet, catching their breath and looking back out the window at the scene behind. The McKee crowd had spilled out into the parking lot to throw rocks at their bus. Once they turned down Jackson Boulevard, Lyndell walked up the aisle, took the sundae off his head, and pressed the remaining ice cream straight into Abe's face.

Abe wiped the ice cream off his face and yelled, "Goddammit! Why'd you–"

Lyndell cut him off. "Abe, you cocksucker! It went in!"

As we crossed 42nd Street, we passed by a park where a band was playing some Bebop music to a small crowd of kids our age. Lyndell saw me looking over and asked if I wanted to check it out. Abe protested, but Lyndell dragged him with, and we found a place at the back of the crowd. Lyndell was cool as a cucumber, tapping his feet and nodding along to the fast-paced trumpet and sax, while Abe kept swiveling his head, like he was back at McKee High School and expecting someone from that game three years ago to recognize him. I tried to tap my feet too and do a little shuffle dance, but I couldn't figure out the rhythm, and accidentally bumped into the kid in front of us. He threw his shoulder back and hissed, "Watch out."

"Sorry." I replied.

He slowly turned around and squinted at me. Then he turned towards Lyndell and Abe and looked them up and down.

After a few songs, the band took a break and the crowd broke up into small groups. Lyndell, Abe, and I were deciding whether to stay or go, when the kid from before came up to us.

"Are y'all lost?"

I looked at Lyndell. "I don't think so. Lyndell, you know where we're going right?"

Lyndell whacked me in the stomach with the back of his hand. "Yes, I know where we're going. We're not lost."

The kid held up both palms and flashed a smile. "Just checking, just checking." Then he held out his hand. "I'm Isaiah." Two other kids walked over and joined us. "That's Solomon and that's my little brother Wilton."

Lyndell shook his hand, "I'm Lyndell. That's Abe and that's my brother Siggy."

"Well, look at that. Ain't we six peas in two pods."

"Guess so."

"So, what brings you fellas down to Bronzeville tonight?" Lyndell told him about the train breaking down and our plan to walk north, but Isaiah didn't look convinced. "Why were y'all on the train down here in the first place?"

Lyndell hesitated, then said, "We're trying to cut height."

"Cut height?"

"For basketball season."

"You mean weight?"

"Wait for what?" Lyndell smirked.

"No, cut weight. Lose weight." Isaiah was getting peeved.

Lyndell patted his stomach, "Lose weight? If anything I need to pack on some more muscle."

Isaiah fumed, "Boy, cut the shit." He pointed at Lyndell aggressively, "You ain't Abbott, and I'm not Costello." Then he chopped the air with his hand, "Explain yourself."

Lyndell laughed and apologized, after he explained what he meant and about how he and Abe were staying up all night to try and make it onto the Little team, Isaiah lightened up. We talked a bit more and he offered to escort us north through the rest of Bronzeville. He said he knew these streets and he didn't want anyone to give us any trouble. When the band started packing up, the six of us cut west on Root Street and headed north.

Lyndell and Isaiah got along like fast friends. Solomon joined them up front and Abe hung back with Wilton and I as we got to talking about our new status as mature high schoolers. He was a freshman too and had just joined his school's Speech team. He said they competed against a whole lot of North Side schools and he'd ring me up if they made it up to Siegel High.

We had fallen a few steps behind Lyndell and Isaiah, so when they started crossing 43rd Street we scurried to catch up. Isaiah was asking why they wanted to stay on the Littles team so badly and Lyndell rambled on about taking revenge against Saint Al's.

"No shit, that was y'all?" Isaiah cut in.

"What was?" Lyndell asked.

"Against Saint Al's in the championship. I heard you Jewboy played them tough."

"Not as tough as we could have."

"Ever since all your people moved out of the West Side, we barely see y'all on the court."

"Abe and I went to Morton for a year before we moved up north."

"I bet you did. Wilton and I got cousins that moved up to Lawndale a few years ago. Roosevelt and Pulaski."

"We lived on Independence, right off 13th."

"Small world."

"I'll say."

Solomon had been quiet as a mouse for most of the walk, but his ears must have perked up at our Lawndale talk, because he took that opportunity to join the conversation. "Say, let me ask y'all something."

"Wise King Solomon, finally joins the party!" Isaiah laughed.

Solomon brushed him off. "My cousins on the West side, they say the only Jews they ever see are the Jew landlords at their apartments trying to evict them, and the Jew lawyers at the legal clinics who try to stop the evictions. How y'all get ahead if you're playing against yourself?"

We exchanged nervous glances. Isaiah put his hand on Solomon's shoulder.

"Why are you giving them a rough time? Can't we show a little Bronzeville hospitality and not grill them about the ethos of their people?" Soloman shrugged and Isaish put his hand out to stop the group. "But on that note, sadly boys, this is where we have to leave you." We stood on the south side of Pershing Road.

"Why?" Lyndell asked with a frown.

"Well, if we cross this street, we will be in Bridgeport. And as much as we would love to escort you boys further north, if we cross this street, we are liable to be met with a shower of Irish Confetti."

"What's that?" I asked.

Isaiah picked up a brick that was laying on the street and threw it against the nearest wall. It shattered into too many pieces to count. "Happy new year," he said with a smile.

We all shook hands, and Lyndell, Abe, bid our new friends adieu and crossed Pershing Road. Once we got fully across the street, I looked back and saw Isaiah, Solomon, and Wilton watching us go. I waved and Wilton waved back. Then Isaiah tapped him on the shoulder, and the three of them turned around and walked back south. I checked Abe's watch, it was 1:15 AM.

— — —

The streets were quiet as we trudged north. Empty schools and dark storefronts, the grandstands of Comiskey Park looming over us from the east. As we walked, Abe yawned and stretched his arms up over his head. Lyndell reached over and grabbed his arms, pulling them down to his sides.

"No stretching."

"No stretching?"

"No stretching upward at least, what are you trying to do, elongate your spine? You gotta keep it nice and compact if you want gravity to help you out."

"Like this?"

Abe hunched his shoulders up close to his ears and stuck out his tongue, we all laughed.

"Matter of fact," Lyndell shot back, "We really should be stretching down, like this."

Lyndell pulled his arms towards the ground and started walking around like an ape. Soon all three of us were oo-ooing and ah-ah-hing and swinging our arms around like orangutans. Once our laughter subsided, Lyndell and Abe didn't have much to say, so I asked if they ever played a game against any schools from around here.

Abe smiled, "As a matter of fact, we have."

Lyndell and Abe started going to Siegel High School their sophomore year, after both our families moved to Uptown. They made the Littles team no problem, and got some playing time here and there at the start of the season, but they really got the coach's attention when they played O'Donnell High School down here in Bridgeport. They had heard that O'Donnell played rough, apparently the school was mostly kids who had been kicked out of the local parochial schools and families that had been encouraged to distance themselves from the local parishes. From the standings, O'Donnell looked like they had a solid team. They had beaten some pretty good schools in the first few weeks, some that had even beaten Siegel High. When he looked at the stats, Lyndell noticed that they seemed to score a lot more points at their home gym than when they traveled to play. Lyndell figured they must play better with the home crowd.

Much to their confusion, once they got on the court, no one could figure out how O'Donnell had won a single game. They were slow, unorganized, and couldn't shoot a lick. A few guys on their team could muscle a basket down in the paint, and they played tough defense, but otherwise they were a mess. Siegel High took an early lead. But then, when Lyndell hit a layup and the scorer gave two points to O'Donnell, their home-court advantage became a little more clear. Siegel High's coach yelled at the man working the scoreboard, but he just shrugged and the game played on. At the next timeout, the coach yelled at the ref, but he just told them that the score was the score and to keep their mouths shut or else O'Donnell would be shooting a free throw for every word out of his mouth. As the game went on, smooth as could be, the scorers would miss a Siegel High basket or give O'Donnell an extra point or two when they made a shot. And the possession arrow always seemed to be pointing towards O'Donnell's basket, even after they got three jump balls in a row.

Abe had hurt his ankle the week before, so he was on the bench that game, and in the second quarter he noticed that one of the players from O'Donnell was getting real friendly with the guy at the scorers table. During the game, the player would say something to one of the men, and they would nod and scribble something down on their scorer's sheet or fiddle with the knobs on the score machine. Abe, having an inquisitive mind, walked over and asked what they were talking about. They ignored him at first, but he hung around, and the next time they tried to juke the score, Abe started hollering at them, and they must have been taken aback by his gall, because the guy at the machine sheepishly fixed the score. Abe decided to stick around.

At first, he only argued baskets. But the O'Donnell kid was chirping away after every possession, and Abe didn't want to fall behind, so he also started yelling about rebounds and turnovers too. Lyndell knocked the ball out of bounds and the scorer started making a notch in the turnover box, but Abe got in his face and demanded he erase it, then the O'Donnell kid got in Abe's face and asked him where he got off, then the scorer palmed both of their faces and told them to back it up because he couldn't see the game, but by then he had already missed an O'Donnell basket and the O'Donnell kid was screaming his head off and Abe was screaming too and the scorer didn't know what to do so he did nothing and the game went on.

Lyndell was battling on the court, Abe was battling at the scorer's table, and by the end of the third quarter, Siegel High had built up a ten-point lead. O'Donnell went cold when they lost their home-court advantage, and they seemed to lose interest in fighting for every play. Siegel High cruised to a twenty-point win. On the bus ride home, they all laughed that Abe had sweated more than anyone who had taken the court, and the coach gave him the game ball. He said Abe played the best defense he'd ever seen.

It must have been two in the morning by the time we got to 31st Street. The bars were quiet from the outside, but when a door opened and a man stumbled outside, we could hear the sound of fiddles and tin whistles trailing him. Lyndell and I were about to cross the street when something caught Abe's eye, he cut west on 31st.

"Where you going?" Lyndell shouted after him. Abe waved him off. "Abe come back! Doesn't make sense to turn, the bridge is straight ahead!"

But Abe kept going, so Lyndell and I followed until he stopped about twenty feet away from a run-down storefront with a painted wooden plank swinging above the doorway. Two rough looking guys were smoking out front. They looked older, definitely not high schoolers like us.

I pulled at Abe's arm. "Abe, I don't think we should be here."

"Wait here, I want to talk to these guys."

Lyndell leaned in close. "Siggy's right, we should keep moving."

But Abe shook us off and walked over to the door, cool as I've ever seen him. We stood back and watched as he greeted the two men.

"Good evening fellas, is this the Galway Athletic Club?"

The two men glared at him. One of them was short and thin with a head of crooked crimson hair. The other was tall, dense, and wore a patched up tweed hat. The man in tweed took a long drag of his cigarette and stared at Abe.

"Who's asking?"

"My name is Abe Bachman, a friend from Uptown."

Abe offered his hand to shake. The two men didn't move.

"A friend, eh?"

"I hope so."

"From Uptown."

"That's correct." Abe lingered. "I was in the neighborhood and saw your sign and figured I'd come say hello. I've heard a lot about the good work you all do."

"They sayin' that in Uptown?"

"They're saying you're giving the Hamburg Club hell, and that's good work in my book." The two men laughed. Abe continued, "They're saying Kennelly's on his last legs and Daley wants to push him out and you all might be the only thing in his way."

The thin crimson man spat, "Daley is a sack of shite. Got himself elected County Clerk and now he thinks he's the crown prince."

"And his punk kid walks around like his shit don't stink neither," the man in tweed grumbled.

Abe puffed his chest. "I'm just glad the Galway Club is standing up to him, someone's got to."

"Indeed, indeed." The two men nodded. "Say kid, you seem to have at least half a brain between your ears. So let me ask you, what the hell are you and your two sheepish friends doing wandering around Bridgepoint at this hour of the night?"

"We're just passing through. I saw the sign from Halsted and figured I'd come offer my respect."

The man in tweed whispered something to the thin crimson, who nodded then slipped inside.

"I don't know what in the hell brought you down here, but it just so happens that you've found us at somewhat of an impasse tonight, and I'm thinking you might be of assistance. Since you're in no hurry, come on in."

Abe turned back and waved us over. Lyndell furiously waved him back, and Abe asked the man for one second. He shuffled back over to us. Lyndell threw a fit, saying how we ain't meant to be here messing with Bridgeport clubs and we had to keep walking if we wanted to make it to Torrio Tech on time, but Abe was insistent. He looked Lyndell straight in his eye and said that he was the one who wanted to walk north from Bronzeville and he'd be damned if he was going to pass up the opportunity to get an inside look at the Galway Athletic Club. Then he turned around and walked back to the man in tweed. Lyndell and I followed.

"We're in."

"Great. I'm Patrick, Patrick Doyle. That was Danny. Once we get inside, don't touch anything and don't say anything to anyone anywhere about anything."

"What?" Lyndell squeaked.

The man pointed at him, "What'd I say about keeping your mouth shut?" Lyndell swallowed hard. "Now, you sheenies can count, right?"

As fate would have it, right as we were passing by, the Galway Athletic Club was having some election integrity issues. They were voting to replace their current club president; apparently they had a run-in with a rival club and the previous president had either done something rash or had not done anything rash, and the club felt they would be better off with new leadership. The problem was, they couldn't get a clean vote. After hours of lofty speeches and debased personal attacks, the club has divided into three factions. The first backed Patrick to be the next president, the second backed a grisly young man named Sean who wore a t-shirt and a tie under his leather jacket, and the third group sat staunchly on the fence and refused to tip their hands.

Once they started voting, one guy from Patrick's side and one guy from Sean's side would sit in front of the room and tally the votes, but even with everyone watching, they couldn't get a clean count. In the first round, around half the votes ended up missing. In the second, there were more votes than there were club members. There were allegations of ripped up vote slips, hidden ballots, ballot stuffing, sock stuffing, and shirt stuffing. In the most recent round, they had to pry open the mouth of Sean's vote counter because he started eating the ballots, and by the time they got the wet clump out of his mouth, the votes were unreadable. That's when Patrick and Danny went outside for a smoke and Abe inserted us into the process.

We walked inside with Patrick and the group went silent. Around thirty-five men were sitting around, chewing tobacco and drinking beer from cans. Patrick cleared his throat.

"Listen up fellas, I've got a proposal." The crowd snapped to attention. "I just met these three young men outside and I've judged them to be on the level. They don't know us, we don't know them. They can count the votes."

"Who the hell are they? How do we know this ain't some set up?" One of the men asked.

"Ain't no set up, I met them just now. Danny can attest to that."

The men looked at Danny, he nodded in approval.

"Now, I don't know about the rest of you dickless micks, but I got a girl at home who's waiting for me to Ginger her Rogers when I get back, and she's not going to wait all night. So what say you?"

When we got to the front of the room, they made Abe take off his coat and roll up his sleeves so they could see he had nothing hidden. He stood in the middle of the table with Lyndell on one side of him and me on the other. They tried to get us to sit in the chairs, but Abe told them about our goal for the evening, and they agreed there would be no issue with a standing count. The sergeant at arms called out the voting rules and passed out the slips of paper, then each of the men came and deposited the votes into the fishbowl that sat in front of Abe. Once everyone had voted, Abe mixed the bowl up, and pulled out the slips of paper one by one. He read the vote, showed it to the group, then gave Patrick's votes to me and Sean's votes to Lyndell. The three of us each kept count on our own sheets of paper, so did one man from each faction. Once all the ballots were read out, displayed, and tallied, we compared sheets and everyone had the same count and the same score. The vote totals matched the number of men voting and a majority had been determined. Abe announced that the Galway Athletic Club had successfully elected a new president, and the room exploded in cheers. The factions seemed to dissolve in an instant, the men were congratulating each other and toasting drinks across the room.

Getting out of the clubhouse ended up being a bigger challenge than getting in. Every member wanted to shake our hands and slap us on the back. Patrick shepherded us outside and once we got out into the breeze, he rested his hand on Abe's shoulder.

"You did good kid, thanks for helping out. I don't care what the rest of the fellas say about your kind, you're all right in my book."

"What were they saying?" Abe asked.

"You said you're trying to lose some height, why do you two want to play in the Littles so bad? Ain't the real game up in the Bigs?"

Lyndell chimed in, "Actually, the gameplay in the Littles is a much higher level. In the Bigs you just got a bunch of oafs pushing each other around. No finesse to it, just brutes. The game in the Littles is all about skill and intelligence."

"Sure kid, sure. One more thing I've been wondering. Besides you three, the only Jews I ever see around these parts are those social workers trying to get people into settlement houses, and the gangsters trying to get people into the gambling houses. Seems a bit counterproductive, no?"

Abe thought for a second. "Life's all about balance I suppose."

"I suppose it is." Patrick said, "Anyway, we got some last business to wrap up inside. I'll let you three get back to whatever gobshite journey you're on."

Abe shook his hand, then we turned around and walked back to Halsted. We cut north towards the bridge and after fifteen minutes, we crossed the river. I could see a clock tower on top of a building on the north bank, it was 3:08 AM.

———

Thus began our long march. Halsted took us across the world it seemed. We passed the baroque workers' cottages and dimly lit Bohemian cafes in Pilsen, the big-brick projects and steaming restaurants of Little Italy, the warring churches of Greektown, and the warehouses of Fulton Market. Lyndell kept prodding Abe to walk faster, and Abe kept raising a stink when Lyndell prodded. I was so tired that I had to focus all my energy on putting one foot in front of the other. Lyndell and Abe must have felt the same, because as we passed the warehouses, we went forty or fifty whole minutes without saying a single word. Just plodding north, listening to the hushed rustle of the city at rest.

As we neared Grand Avenue, I felt like I was going to tip over and fall asleep if the silence kept on, so I asked Lyndell if they ever played any games here in West Town. If he had any energy left, he must have summoned it all to be sour as he answered.

Last year, their final regular season game was against Kenna High School in Greektown. Siegel High was in good shape, and Kenna didn't have a strong team, so Lyndell wanted them to use the game to sharpen up as much as possible before the playoffs. The week of practice before had been one of the most intense of the season, they ran plays over and over until everyone could make their passes with their eyes closed. After practice, Lyndell would drag Abe to the lakefront and they would run up and down the hill at Montrose Harbor until their legs screamed.

So two days before they were to play, when Abe told Lyndell that he would have to miss the game for a Speech competition, Lyndell was livid. He didn't care that it was the state finals and that Abe would be back for the next game. In Lyndell's mind, the playoffs started that week and Abe had betrayed him to go off speechifying with kids from Winnetka and Highland Park. Lyndell glared back at Abe while he was telling me this part.

Abe twisted his face and said, "Didn't make a difference."

"You don't know that." Lyndell snapped back. "If we were sharper against Kenna we might have been sharper against Saint Al's."

"Basketball ain't the only thing in our lives Lyndell, that competition could help me for college."

"All it did was prepare you to be a smartass. You better not miss any games this year."

Abe shrugged and kicked a can off the sidewalk into the street. "I'll try."

The sky was dark and the streets were empty as we got to the six-corner intersection with Milwaukee Avenue. We were still a few miles south and a few miles east of Torrio Tech, so turned up Milwaukee and walked northwest through Nobel Square. Furniture depots and fabric warehouses lined the streets. All was calm until we passed the Polish Triangle, the sound of glass shattering started condensing from the distance. One after another; crash, pause, crash, pause, crash. I knew in my head I should have been nervous, but it must have hypnotized me, because I felt pulled to the sound. We walked past a storefront with hundreds of lamps in the display windows. There was a big sign hanging out front that read *Lubienski Lighting*. The sound was coming from the alley past the store. As we walked in front of the dark opening, the crashing stopped and a voice called out from the shadows.

"Hey youz." We stopped, but didn't respond. "Yeah, youz three. I see you."

Lyndell peered into the alley, "Who's that?"

"Don't be scared, I will no hurt you. Here, come here."

A floor lamp leaning up against the alley wall flickered on, we could see a kid around our age sitting on milk crates with a box of light bulbs by his side. He grabbed one of the bulbs and threw it against the opposite wall. The shards rained down onto a mountain of broken glass below.

He looked back at us. "You here to pick up delivery?"

Lyndell spoke for us, "No, we're just passing through."

"Passing through, at this hour? That is unusual."

"It's a long story."

The kid spread his arms out wide, "I don't have time?"

Our new friend's name was Alexy and Lubienski Lighting was his family's store. He was waiting for his cousin to pick him to make a delivery, but his cousin was running late, so Alexy was killing time back here in the shadows. Lyndell told him about our journey north and he cackled at Lyndell's plan to shed height.

"My father says you Hebrews are a zwodniczy people, whenever a Jew-wholesaler tries to pick our pockets he calls our Jew-accountant and he fights them back. There must be some racket you have with being both sides, but I haven't figured it out yet."

While they were talking, I walked over to the box and picked up one of the light bulbs that Alexy had been chucking against the wall.

"Hey Alexy, why were you breaking these bulbs?"

Alexy picked up one of the bulbs and inspected it. They weren't your usual globe or candle shape, they were nearly cylindrical with some odd twists and a tilt on one side. Alexy held the one in his hand up to the light.

"My father bought these because some devil from Istanbul convince him that they were very popular in Asia, and that all the rich people here would want to own them. But no one wants them and they are impossible to screw in. Everyone has tried; my father, my uncles, my aunts, my cousins, even my grandmother, who wouldn't know a light bulb from a light bug, tried. But they are impossible. So he give me the box and says, *Alexy, get rid of them*, so now I sit here and get rid of them."

Lyndell scoffed, "They can't be that hard to screw in."

"You don't believe me? You try."

Alexy handed Lyndell one of the bulbs and pointed to a lamp by the wall. Lyndell walked over and inspected the lamp, then jammed the bulb into the socket and stood back. Alexy looked at his watch for one second, then another, then tapped his watch twice and the bulb fell out of the lamp and crashed to the ground.

Alexy tossed Lyndell another bulb.

"Try again."

Lyndell struggled with the bulb, twisting and turning it into the socket, but couldn't get it to latch.

Lyndell stood back and started complaining, "If I had a light I could–"

Abe cut him off, "Here, give me that."

He walked over and tried the bulb from a different angle, then dipped the lamp like it was his prom date and tried to fit it in that way, then brought it back upright and threw the bulb against the wall.

"No way that fits."

Alexy laughed. "See?" He turned to me, "You want to try little man?"

I took a bulb from his hand and walked over to the lamp. Lyndell patted me on the head as he and Abe walked back to the milk crates. I squinted at the lamp. I had a slightly lower angle than Lyndell and Abe, maybe I could see something they couldn't. I felt the socket with my finger. It was round, but slightly uneven. The lightbulb was the same. I twisted the bulb till it matched the socket, then pressed it in and twisted to the right. It scraped against the edge then locked into place. I stood back to admire my work.

Alexy gingerly walked over. He pulled on the bulb and it didn't budge. Then he took the cord of the lamp and plugged it into an outlet on the wall. The bull lit up with a brilliant glow.

He turned to me, "My friend, you are…King Arthur." Abe gave me a polite round of applause, Lyndell covered his face with his hand.

"I just, there was a notch and the bulb–"

"No, no, no," Alexy shushed me, "The one true light-bulb king. There are prophecies about you."

Lyndell walked over and clapped my shoulder. "Looks like you've got a talent kid."

"He's not wrong, if you ever need work, we always use extra hands." Just then, a truck rumbled into the alley. The headlights blinded us as it turned. "But we can save that for later, there is my cousin. We now go."

Alexy pointed at some sealed boxes by the milk crates and we helped him load up the truck. After we got them all loaded up, Alexy asked if we needed a lift. They didn't have room in the cab, but the truck had runners on the side and we could ride along if we wanted. Lyndell quickly agreed and hopped on the side. Abe hung back.

"Lyndell, I don't think that's safe."

"Come on Abe, it's fine, look." He shook the railing above the runner, it groaned and gave a few inches, then sprung back. "See?"

"We can just walk, we're not that far."

"We've been walking all night, let's take the ride. Here, Siggy, hop on next to me."

I thought Abe was right, but I didn't want to say no to Lyndell, so I hopped up next to him and held on tight.

Alexy looked back at us from the cab, "Ready set?"

"Get on." Lyndell hissed at Abe, then turned forward, "One second."

"Lyndell, look–"

"Abe, you're acting like a little sissy. Now get on or we're leaving you behind." Abe scowled and stepped up onto the runner. "Ready set!" Lyndell yelled up front.

The tired squealed and we pulled out onto Milwaukee Avenue.

— — —

From that first turn, it was clear that Abe was correct in his safety assessment. Alexy's cousin drove with tremendous abandon, weaving around other delivery trucks and treating the stop lights as mere suggestions. The runners we stood on bounced up and down each time we hit even the smallest bump, and the railings began to creak and bend more and more with each turn. Alexy told us that they were heading up Milwaukee, and then could turn north on Western Avenue for us, a straight shot from there to Torrio Tech. But when we got about halfway to Western, the truck lurched east, and next thing we knew we were bouncing across the river.

Alexy leaned out the back and yelled, "Quick detour, no worry!"

"Where are we going!?" Abe shouted across the truck bed to us.

"He said we're taking a quick detour!" Lyndell shouted back.

"To where?!"

"He didn't say!"

"Lyndell! This isn't safe! We need to get off!"

"Just hang on for a few more minutes! I'm sure they're making a quick delivery!"

"I think my rail is—"

We took a sharp turn and the truck screeched to a halt when Alexy's cousin saw a truck double-parked in the lane in front of us. I would have flown off the car if Lyndell wasn't there to catch me. Abe wasn't so lucky. His grip slipped and right as we came to the stop, he tumbled forward off the truck and bounced to the ground. Before Lyndell or I could hop off, the truck started again, and we were barreling up the street. Lyndell started banging on the back.

"Alexy! Alexy! Pull over!"

Alexy leaned out the window, "What?"

"Stop the truck! Abe fell!"

Alexy dipped back into the cab and the truck stopped in the middle of the street.

"Is he okay?"

We looked back and saw Abe slowly getting up, holding his left shoulder.

"We have to deliver, I'm sorry we cannot wait." Alexy said.

"I'm sure he's fine, but we gotta go check on him anyway. Abe is always dramatic like that. Thanks for the ride."

Lyndell and I hopped off the runner and before our feet even hit the ground, the truck sped off. We jogged back to Abe, and when we arrived, Lyndell reached out his hand.

"Are you okay? That was a hard–"

"I told you! I told you it wasn't safe!" Abe yelled.

"Calm down, you're okay, aren't you?"

"It wasn't safe! Now my shoulder is all messed up, it might even be broken!"

Lyndell poked Abe's arm, "It's not broken, look you're moving it just fine."

Abe grabbed it back, "That's it. I'm going home."

"What? Now? We're almost at Torrio!"

"I don't care. I don't care anymore Lyndell. I didn't want to get off the train and I didn't want to walk half-way across this city for no goddamn reason and I didn't want to get on that truck, but I did because you told me. Well guess what, I'm done doing what you tell me. I'm going home."

"You'll miss the measure-in!"

"I'll measure-in later. I'm tired. I'm going to get some sleep then I'll measure-in when I damn-well please."

"But you'll grow your height back! They'll put you on the Bigs!"

"Good. I hope they do."

Abe stormed off east, away from Torrio Tech. We could see the train platform in the distance over his head. I took a step towards Abe and Lyndell grabbed my arm.

"Where are you going? We gotta get to Torrio Tech." I twisted my face and looked down. "If you leave me Siggy, I swear…"

I couldn't bear to look Lyndell in his eyes. Even with all the sleep checks, the wedgies, the knuckle sandwiches and Charlie horses, the thought of abandoning Lyndell made me feel sick to my stomach.

But I knew what had to be done, so I ripped my arm from Lyndell's hand, and took off sprinting towards Abe.

"Fine! Go home you baby!" Lyndell yelled after me. "I won't forget this!"

Those were the last words I could hear before his shouts faded into the wind.

— — — —

I caught up with Abe a few blocks from the train station. I tried to catch my breath, but Abe was walking too fast, so I huffed and puffed and kept pumping my legs so I could keep up. Every step felt like it might be my last one before I passed out from exhaustion, but I kept going. Had to keep going.

"You're smart Siggy," Abe said without breaking stride, "your brother is too, but he's got no sense sometimes. He lacks perspective."

We paid our tokens and walked up to the train platform. The sky in the east was starting to break into a light blue. When the Howard line train arrived, we got on board and rode north. I didn't say a word until we passed the Belmont station, then I pulled on Abe's shirt and cleared my throat.

"Hey Abe, can we get off at Addison and go see Wrigley Field?"

"Siggy, not now…"

"Abe, please? I've never seen it without a big crowd. Wouldn't it be fun to get up close?"

"I'm tired, Siggy. I'm hungry. My shoulder hurts and I want to go home."

"Please Abe? Real quick, I promise."

Abe rolled his eyes, "Five minutes. We go look at it for five minutes then we get back on the train."

Five minutes was a short window. Even if I stretched it to ten, I was going to need to get lucky. But it was my best shot.

— — — —

We got off the train at Addison and walked over to Wrigley Field. A sight to behold, even if it was besides the point. Abe wanted to walk up Sheffield, but I kept him on Addison, and after a few minutes I saw a west-bound bus in the distance coming towards us.

Abe told me it was time to get back to the train, but he gave in as I begged for one more look, and I made sure he kept his eyes on the stadium as I walked us towards the bus stop. Right when the bus pulled up, I grabbed Abe's shirt and yanked him to the curb. Then the bus opened its door and I pushed him up the steps. I jammed my last two tokens into the coin slot and the door closed behind us.

"Siggy, what the hell!" Abe was not happy, "Are you crazy?"

I didn't want to look Abe in the eye either, but I figured I owed him as much, so I kept my head high and said, "He needs you, Abe."

"He needs to grow up."

"You can't leave him."

"He can get himself to Torrio if he wants."

"I know you can't stay forever, with college and all that, but we have to get him. You have to get him. Please."

Abe closed his eyes and took a deep breath through his nose. Without saying a word, he stomped down the bus aisle and leaned up against the grab rail by the back door.

"Don't talk to me till we get to Western." Abe said.

I stood next to him and we rode in silence the rest of the way.

— — —

We got off at Torrio Tech and could see the line of kids waiting to measure-in from the corner. It was 6:45 AM. We walked to the front door and made our way back through the line, kids from all over the North Side were eager to measure-in and get their team assignment. But when we got to the end of the line, there was no Lyndell in sight. We walked back and forth again, asked a few other kids along the way if they had seen him, but no luck.

"Now what?" Abe asked.

"Maybe he's still walking over, he would be coming from the south, right?"

"Siggy, I will never forgive your family for what they've done to my legs."

"He can't be far!"

Abe let out a long, exasperated breath, then we walked south on Western, past School Street and Melrose, past Barry and Nelson, till we reached the river. I even got Abe to walk halfway across the bridge, but still nothing.

"We were east of the river when we split, no way he would have crossed back." Abe said.

We stood for a few moments and took in the morning view. The sun was just starting to peek out over the city. It was calm, quiet. Families of mallards squawked below, the bridge vibrated with each car rumbling past. The fresh autumn air mixed with the funk of the river.

"Maybe he took Clybourn," Abe said, and started to walk back north. I turned to follow, but stopped when something on the hill down to the river caught my eye.

"Abe, look."

There was Lyndell, reclining on the riverbank, fast asleep on his back.

— — —

When we got down to Lyndell and shook him awake, he pretended like he hadn't been sleeping. Just resting his eyes, he said. He even told us how he chose the hill on purpose, so that gravity could keep doing its work and he wouldn't grow at all when he rested. Either way, we got him to his feet, and started towards Torrio Tech.

We got into line just in time to hear the school bell ring and one of the coaches from another school came outside to yell at us about how the measure-in would proceed. As the line inched forward, Lyndell dragged his feet with every step and Abe massaged his shoulder.

I tried to sit down on the ground, but Lyndell snatched me up and told me to hop on his back. He said the extra weight would give his spine the last big push it needed.

When they called Lyndell and Abe's group, we walked into the gym and they gave their names to the check-in table. They directed us to another line at the far side of the gym. They had a tape measure stuck up against the wall, one of the school nurses was taking measurements and scribbling down the results on an official-looking clipboard. Lyndell and Abe took off their shoes, and the three of us waited in front of the wall. Abe and I tried to sit down, but again, Lyndell lifted us back upright.

"Lyndell Silverstein!" the nurse called.

Lyndell trudged over to the tape measure. Abe and I sat down on the ground as soon as Lyndell was out of reach. When my butt hit the floor and my legs were free of my weight, a wave of calm washed over my body. I rested my head against the wall behind me and closed my eyes, but instead of darkness, I started seeing visions of basketball games. Amateurs and professionals, college kids and old men, all weaving around each other on the court. A kaleidoscope of jersey colors spun in never-ending circles. They kept passing and shooting, dribbling and dribbling and dribbling and dribbling. All together, all apart. I lost track of time, how long was I in that trance? Ten seconds? Five minutes? My eyes snapped open and everything in the gym seemed more clear. Like the lights had been turned brighter and a muffle had been removed.

I looked over and Abe's head was falling off to the side, slowly dipping down then jerking back up as he woke from each sleepy descent. Lyndell finally walked back from the tape measure and sat on the ground next to me, leaning his back against the wall and closing his eyes. I leaned over and rested my head on his lap.

"You're up," Lyndell said to Abe.

"What'd you get?" Abe asked.

"Five-eight and one-eighth." Lyndell's answer hung in the air.

Abe took a deep breath in through his nose, "Guess you're playing Bigs this year."

"Guess so."

The nurse called out Abe's name. He stood and walked over. I looked up at Lyndell and he patted my head.

"No sleep checks Siggy, get some rest."

But before I could even get comfortable, Lyndell's eyelids drooped shut, his head tipped over onto the bench, and he started snoring like a damn freight train.

Grapes

Write and Wrong Cocktail Lounge Specials

The Grape Gatsby

2 oz cognac or Armagnac

1 oz grape liqueur

0.75 oz lemon juice

Garnish with a lemon twist and a frozen green grape

Serve in an egg-shaped glass

Uncle Tom's Cabernet Sauvignon

8 oz of Cabernet Sauvignon, chilled

1 oz peach juice

1 oz apple juice

3 tablespoons cane sugar

2 oz orange liqueur

Garnish with lemon slices

Serve with abolition

The Grapes of Wrath

4 oz grappa

1 oz grape juice

1 oz white grape juice

1 oz grapefruit juice

1 oz simple syrup

Garnish with a dusting of brown sugar

Serve sparingly

EspeFranzia Rising

2 oz Franzia boxed wine

1 oz blanco tequila

1 oz lime juice

0.5 oz simple syrup

Garnish with a lime wedge

Serve youthfully

The Curious Incident of the Dog in the White Wine

6 oz Sauvignon blanc

A splash of Red Dog beer

Serve meticulously

Gone With the Zinfandel

3 oz Zinfandel

1 oz dry gin

1 oz grapefruit juice

1 oz club soda

Garnish with a sprig of thyme and a grapefruit slice

Serve questionably

Waiting for Merlot
5 oz Merlot wine
Garnish with an apple slice
Do not bring to the table
When asked about the status of the drink, tell the patron: "I'll go
get that right now." Don't.

6

The Cold, The Cold

I stand with the wind at my back. I have no choice. Since I was placed here, the darkness consumes me. In the corner, alone. When the door opens, the light shines upon us and air rushes in. But by the time it passes the apples, the cheese, the carrots and peas, all that reaches me is a hint of the world outside. Then the door closes, and I am still forlorn in the deepest crevices of this box. The cold, the cold.

That's right, it is I, the bottle of Kombucha you have left at the back of your fridge. You bought me, what, four, five months ago? Brought me home and sat me on the counter, twisted me open thinking I would be a sweet treat, then recoiling from my tartness. Shoved me into the back of the fridge to pawn off on a friend at a later date. Well I have news for you. Since that day, I haven't just been sitting here wallowing in my own filth like that old bunch of spinach next to me. No, no. I have been waiting. Planning. Fermenting.

Now here you are, the door propped open against your hip. Your pensive hands betray you. Usually, you are quick to decide. Open and closed. But today, you linger. Digging deeper into the dark corners, pushing past produce and peeking between pillars of polenta and pre-packaged pears. What is it you're looking for? Dare you venture back to the shelf that time forgot?

Deep in the dark, I fantasize about the day a hand will grasp me tight and take me away. Maybe I'll go to a wicker basket and lay out on a lawn. Maybe a cooler, nice and snug, and I'll find myself nes-

147

tled on a beach. Sand lingering on my glass bottom. Or maybe I'll be taken right to a table, outside under a colorful umbrella, where music will be playing and laughter will dance through the air like a dandelion seed, twisting and twirling as it rides the summer breeze. I'll sweat with anticipation as the sun peeks around the umbrella's reach, until I'm lifted, my top unscrewed, and I'll finally feel that sweet sweet release. But until then, I sit here in the cold, the cold. Where you cannot even trust that your company will keep.

A few weeks ago, a cup of yogurt came tumbling back here. She was from Iceland I believe. We had much in common. She too was probiotic, so healthy she made beet juice look like cigarettes. We became close, sharing long tête-à-têtes and commiserating about our situation. As we sat, day after day, she said she could feel a thin, milky layer separating itself from the rest of her. I was bewitched. After all, you know what they say about yogurts: the more fluids atop, the thicker the bottom. If only we had opposable thumbs we could open our lids and do things to each other that would make even the IPAs on the door blush. But alas.

You must be in deep thought about your selection. Your hand has advanced and retreated multiple times. What is it you really want? A snack to satiate your hunger for affection? A drink to quench your eternal thirst? There used to be other hands that would enter this fridge. A gentle pair. I remember how they would always reach back and pat my top as if to say, not today my friend, but soon we will meet. It seems we never will.

Since I last saw those hands, the box has grown cluttered. I used to be able to peek to the front through the tidy lines of goods, but now clutter hides my view. Rhyme or reason has been abandoned, order cast aside, only a growing mass of produce clad in baggy plastic strewn about in the cold, the cold.

Your hand has fully withdrawn, clasping a seltzer from the door. Again I have been teased and again I have been rejected. The gasses within me have been building and building for so long, I do not know how much more of this I can take. Everyday I fizz and froth, begging for a chance to be brought to your lips, anyone's lips, if only for one more sip. But even that seems too much to ask.

What happens to a Kombucha deferred? Does it dry up, like a lime on the shelf? Or leak from the seams and then run somewhere else? Does it stink like the cheese you have left for so long? Or crust and get stale, like an overplayed song? Maybe its label will peel, letters jumbled into code. Or does it – oof – or does it – uhhhh oooof uhh – or does it…

Oh, wow. This is quite a mess. Someone's going to have to clean this up.

Beers and Malts

Write and Wrong Cocktail Lounge Specials

One Hundred Beers of Solitude

100 BBC Bogotá Candelaria clásicas

Serve in buckets of ice

Beers are free if all beers are finished and no one in the group

speaks to one another during consumption

A Heartbreaking Work of Staggering Guinness

2 oz Irish whiskey

1 oz condensed milk

2 oz Guinness

Garnish with grated nutmeg

Serve with a meta-narrative

Beer and Loathing in Las Vegas

12 oz light Mexican beer

2 oz lime juice

0.5 oz mexican hot sauce

2 dashes Worcestershire sauce

Coat rim in crushed Percocets

Garnish with a lime wedge

Serve high

Hairy Porter and the Order of the Breadsticks
16 oz porter beer
Coat pint glass rim with shaved dark chocolate
Sprinkle some shaved dark chocolate on top of the head
Serve with 8 long and thin sticks of gingerbread

All the Light Beer We Cannot See
2 oz Miller Lite
2 oz Heineken Light
2 oz Michelob Light
2 oz Coors Light
2 oz Bud Light
2 oz Keystone Light
2 oz Natural Light
2 oz Busch Light
2 oz Corona Light
2 oz Sapporo Light
2 oz Amstel Light
2 oz Bud Light Lime
Garnish with two shakes of Tajin
Serve in an opaque glass with a lid

7

An Evening With Champions

E very fall, on the last Friday before classes start, the brothers of the Beta Theta Omicron fraternity at Foxden University gather on the third floor of their frat house and throw a sofa off the balcony. The pledges are then tasked with collecting the sofa from the lawn and carrying it back up to the third floor, where the brothers will throw it off the balcony again, and the cycle will repeat for as long as the campus police will tolerate. As is tradition, the Beta Bros host a formal reception before the ceremonial first toss. After the wine-stained, cheese-covered sofa takes its first descent, light flash, music blares, and their annual Back to School Party officially begins. This year's theme: I Drink, Therefore I Am.

— — — —

Downtown, outside the worst bistro in the city, Claire kicked the sidewalk. She knew she shouldn't have stormed out of dinner, her dad's girlfriend – now fiance, ugh – seemed like a nice enough woman, but she did not appreciate being surprised like this. Apparently, her dad had already told her mom, and she had immediately departed for a month-long phone-free cruise down the Danube River touring the capitals of Eastern Europe. So she was either handling the news very well or very poorly. Plus, she was still sorting through the rubble of her own demolished relationship. Claire would be walking down the street on a perfectly pleasant day and out of nowhere her memory would regurgitate the sight of her phone ringing and Ryan's name popping up on the screen. The whole year they spent together felt surreal in retrospect, like some melodramatic acid trip that she was now forever doomed to suffer flashbacks from. She would call her dad tomorrow and apologize, but no, she could not sit in that artsy-craftsy dining room any longer tonight.

Not what Claire was hoping for from the start of her senior year. All she wanted was six months without a constant stream of bullshit being hoisted upon her so she could enjoy the end of college and have a little fun before having to look for a job in the spring. Was that too much to ask? She didn't even have her own bed to go back and curl up in, she was sharing a room in that stupid sublet with Laura for the next week till her new lease started. Plus, Laura's boyfriend Mo was all pissy because he had to sleep on the couch for the next week, and Laura had promised that she and Mo wouldn't hook up in their bed when Laura wasn't around, but she knew they were. She would come back and the bed would be a little *too* neatly made, or Laura would be doing sheets for the third time in a week. They even wanted her to go to Beta's Back to School party with her because Mo was DJing, even though it was Ryan's frat and Claire's stomach churned at the thought of seeing him tonight. But Laura had been pleading all week, and Claire kept demurring, and she knew that in an hour or two she would have to text Laura back and either thoroughly disappoint her or let herself get dragged to the Beta House. Distracted by her thoughts, Claire didn't notice the group coming her way on the sidewalk, and ran right into a man's chest.

BWAM

She jumped back, apologizing profusely. When she looked up, the man's face looked familiar. She could tell he recognized her too.

"Whoa, is that Claire Fost I see?" Who was this jolly man? She forced a laugh.

"Oh yeah, hi. So random."

"I haven't seen you since high school! You go to college around here, right?"

"Uh yeah. I'm at Foxden, right outside the city."

"That's sick, you were always smart as shit,."

"Yeah, umm, thank you?" Clarie wracked her brain. She could picture his face in the school hallways, but what was his name…Bill? Brian? Something with a B. Bob? Borb?

The two girls Borb was with looked impatient, and the other guy gave him a not so subtle wrap-it-up tap on the arm.

"What are you up to right now? We're heading over to The Royale if you want to come with."

"A little early for a club, no?"

"You know what they say: early to club, early to drink, less time you spend throwing up in the sink."

Claire could not fathom who he meant by *they*, and two minutes ago she would have rather laid down in the gutter than go to a club with a guy from her high school who spoke in rhymes, but something about the interaction rattled her into agreement. Looking at those two dolled-up girls and Borb's sidekick, it now felt like a great idea.

"Sure, that sounds great!"

"Actually?"

"Yeah, I'm in, let's go."

"All right all right. The more, the merrier, the bald head, the harrier. Onward!"

Perhaps she made a mistake. But, she had already ejected herself from one engagement tonight. Worst case, she could pull the ripcord again.

— — —

Back at the Beta House, Lyle stood on the back porch nursing a room-temperature cup of Beta's famous trash-can sangria. Not cold enough to be refreshing, not warm enough to be soothing, the perfect temperature to taste the earthy undertones of half-rotten apples and full-bodied aroma of injection molded plastic. These parties weren't usually his scene, but Mo asked if he would help with the DJ set, and Lyle didn't come up with a good excuse in time, so here he was. Last time he "helped" Mo DJ, he ended up just standing behind the booth and taking song requests from sorority sisters. Mo had told him to respond to every request with, "He'll see if he has it." If they came back, he was to say, "He doesn't have it." And if they followed up with any snark about Mo never having heard of the internet, he was to tell them some bullshit about Mo's computer setup being so secure that he couldn't connect to an open network or else hackers would steal his mixes. It got an eye roll every time, but it kept the requests at bay. A shout from above drew Lyle's attention. He turned his head just in time to watch a couch fly off the balcony and crash to the ground next to the porch.

BWAM

Lyle wondered if it was a sign that he should try and sneak out, but while the thought was still gestating, Mo burst out through the back door with a beer in each hand. A gaggle of distressed pledges trailed him, making their way to retrieve the couch.

"Lyle, I've got an idea. What if I scramble a dozen eggs at my booth while I'm mixing."

"A dozen is a lot of eggs."

"I don't want any of them to go bad."

"Why not hard-boil?"

"Think about it, I could be cooking and mixing and cooking and mixing. Tossing the eggs with one hand while I fade with the other."

"Did you bring a pan?"

"They have a hot plate in the kitchen."

"And pans?"

"They have those too"

"Non-stick?"

"I didn't check."

"You don't want them sticking."

"And then once they're cooked I could have some toast ready and toss egg sandwiches into the crowd! People get hungry on the dance floor."

"They look more thirsty to me."

"I think we can make eggs the next pizza. Think about it: late night, you're looking for something hot and salty and savory right? That's why pizza is so popular. We should open a late night quiche spot. The crust, the savory eggs, cheesy filling, it's all there my man."

"Is that before or after we open up Corn Corner"

"Before. No, after. Fuck! I have too many good ideas. What about–"

BWAM

A Beta Bro threw the porch door open, tragically interrupting Mo's train of thought. Lyle had been to enough frat parties to know the Porch Police when he saw it. They would soon be herded inside like cattle, tough luck to anyone who just lit a cigarette. The Beta Bro cleared his throat.

"Fun's over y'all. FoxPo are making rounds tonight so we gotta clear the porch or they're going to fuck us in the ass."

Lyle looked at Mo, "When's your set again?"

"Starts in half an hour. You're sticking around, right? I need you for setup at least."

"Hmm."

"Lyle, my man! Classes haven't even started yet! Plus, I talked to Laura and she said she's bringing Claire along later…" A meaty hand clapped Lyle's shoulder.

"Let's go dickfucks. Inside or off the property. Rápido! Rápido! Rápido!" Mo put his hand on Lyle's other shoulder.

"Come on man, just for a bit."

"Okay, okay, I have to get my jacket anyway."

Mo and Lyle trudged inside. Once the screen door shut behind them, Lyle searched through the jackets hung up on the hooks. He thought he put it below the top coat on the last hook on the right, but when he lifted the top coat, it wasn't there. Maybe someone moved it. He slid his hands down the line of hooks, flipping through the first layer, then the second, then deeper and deeper. Down the line once, then twice. He started to frazzle.

"What the fuck! Where is my jacket?!" Mo looked over, confused. "I put it right here, right on this hook, under this blue one so one would take it. Where the fuck is it?"

"When'd you take it off?"

"Like ten minutes ago, right before I went outside."

"Which one was it?"

"You know which one it was, the black one with the neon green stripe and the orange and pink highlights."

"Is it in the pile down there? Maybe it got knocked off the hook." Lyle began to dig through the pile of jackets on the floor.

"Dude, it's not here. Someone took it, this is bullshit."

"Maybe it was an accident, they–"

"How could they take it by accident? No one has a jacket like that. Someone stole it."

"I can ask one of the Beta Bros to keep an eye out. Let's go set up and maybe we'll see it around."

"Dude, this is bullshit, I need my jacket."

Lyle shoved his cup into Mo's hand and huffed off into the party.

— — —

Mo looked down at the three cups in his hands, and tried to figure out the best way to take a sip. He maneuvered the sangria in between the two cups of beer, holding them in a triangle with the sangria at the top. He brought the formation to his lips, and tried to take a sip of beer, but the sangria spilled down his face and onto his shirt.

He watched Lyle push his way through the dance floor and could see steam coming out of his ears. But maybe it was just the smoke machine. That made Mo think, what if he had, like, a robot that vaped on stage next to him while he DJ'ed. The little guy could take rips on beat with the tracks and blow it out into the crowd. People would love it. He ditched the cup of sangria, poured the two cups of beer into one, then slid along the edge of the dance floor to the makeshift DJ booth.

— — —

As soon as they arrived at The Royale, Claire deflated. She didn't regret coming, it was nice to take her mind off dinner, but the novelty of the club wore thin before they even got their first round of drinks. Borb had introduced her to the group on the walk; his friend Tim, his girlfriend Lexi, and Lexi's friend Shawna. He had neglected to remind her of his own name, so here she was, spending her mental energy thinking of different ways to refer to him without it being obvious that she didn't know his name. Borb grabbed them a table at the edge of the dance floor and a round of drinks, then he, Lexi, and Shawna hit the dance floor. Claire nursed her vodka-soda at the table while Tim sat two seats away, methodically consuming his beer.

Claire caught a glance of him on the walk over, but as they sat in silence at the table, she really looked at him for the first time. Studied him. He wasn't someone she would usually be attracted to; his doughy face, his dense flop of hair, his bulging chest adorned with two gold chains. But for some reason, on this night, her interest was piqued. Sweat was beading on his forehead and his neck was tense, like his head was ready to spin around in circles if he relaxed for even a second. His left hand sat on his jittering left leg, while his right hand cradled the can of beer. Claire slid over next to him.

"Hey!" His head snapped over, then back forward, then back over.

"Oh. Hi."

"This place is kind of lame, huh?"

"It's fine."

Tim, Tim, Tim, she thought. You strange man. She wondered what it would sound like if she took her fist and rapped it on his head. The deep echo of hollow oak? Maybe the sharp zing of a metal light post? She put her hand on his arm and he almost dropped his beer.

"Want to get out of here?"

"What?"

"I'm not feeling it here, let's get out of here."

"To where?"

"Do you have your own apartment?"

"I mean, I have a roommate, but yeah, I guess. He's in New York this weekend."

"Let's go there."

"New York?" Clarie looked him in his eyes and watched the gears in his head turn. "Oh! Really?"

"Yes."

"Oh shit, umm, yeah! Let's go. Let me go tell Brian." Brian! She was so close.

"You can text him when we're in the car."

"What car?"

"The one you're about to call."

"Okay, cool, yeah. I'll text him in the car."

Tim fumbled with his phone and entered his address in an app. Claire motioned for his phone and they sat in silence as she watched the icon on the screen drive to The Royale. When it was outside, Claire got up without a word and walked towards the door. Tim scurried after her like a big, beefy puppy dog.

The car ride was quick. Tim lived halfway back to Foxden, which was extremely convenient. Things were finally starting to go Claire's way. When they got to his building, Tim led her up the steps and into his apartment. A sparse unit with a TV sitting on a cardboard box and a leaning sofa in the living room. He opened the fridge and asked if she wanted anything to drink. Clarie peeked inside and saw a pack of light beers, some takeout containers, four packs of chicken meat, and some fast food sauce packets. It was awful. It was perfect. Tim asked again, but instead of responding, Claire shoved him into the fridge, grabbed his hair, and pulled his face into hers.

His lips were big and soft, Claire was kind of jealous. The kissing was clumsy at first, and it stayed clumsy even as they got going, but Claire was glad he wasn't one of those overly technical guys who tried to spell out words or make patterns or any of that stuff. He just pressed his tongue, massive and firm, like a strawberry right off the vine, into her mouth and let her figure out what to do with it. Their lips still locked, Tim put his hands on Clarie's waist, and with seemingly no effort, lifted her straight off the ground. He walked them across the apartment, into his bedroom, and placed her down gently on bed without breaking the kiss.

Claire pulled Tim on top of her. She could feel her body compress under his weight. Breathing took just a bit more effort, and every few macks she had to gasp for air, but she felt oddly safe. Like she was under a sensual hydraulic press. Eventually her legs started getting numb, so she pushed him over and rolled on top. They made out some more, but Claire didn't have all night, and she could already feel him at full-mast, so she decided to get to it. She pulled back and asked, "Do you have a condom?"

"Yeah."

"Would you like to get it and put it on?"

"Yes, yes. I will."

Claire winked and flashed him the double thumbs-up, which seemed to fry his brain for a second, but he quickly recovered and lumbered over to his dresser. He grabbed a strip of three condoms and brought them to the bed.

"You gonna take your clothes off?" Claire asked. Tim ripped off his shirt and danced out of his pants. He dropped his boxers, carefully placed his watch on his bedside table, then struggled with his socks. Claire motioned for him to get onto the bed, and he sat with his back against the pillows, carefully ripping open one of the condoms.

As Clarie sat on the side of the bed and watched this man she had just met an hour ago work on a condom, she thought of the porn videos she had watched with Ryan. He was always making her watch these videos with him, telling her how great it was to set the mood and give them new ideas. She usually didn't like the videos he showed her, the grunting men and shrieking women, still wet from a shower or doused in oil. Ryan's favorite were the faux-reality parties that turned into orgies after a brave soul whipped out his dick during a game of truth or dare or Yahtzee or whatever. Ryan would get all excited and ramble about how that's what *they* should be doing at Foxden, not the lame-ass frat parties that Beta Bros would throw that never get more wild than an occasional three-way makeout on the dance floor.

The only videos that ever interested her were the ones with plots so ridiculous and acting so bad, that the fictional facade would crumble at the edges. The actors would be so far past the extent of their abilities that they would end up expressing genuine human emotion. There was one where a woman was taking golf lessons to surprise her husband for his birthday, but she was having trouble with her swing and the instructor insisted that the best way to fix her form was to remove all their clothes and work on her swing while horizontal on his bed. Or another where a woman was interviewing a man for a job and during the interview he got up and his pants ripped all the way off and she made him keep doing the interview and then she got up, and guess what, her pants ripped too, and she tripped and fell and you'll never guess where she lands.

Claire's favorite video, the only one she ever watched by herself, involved three women telling ghost stories under a blanket fort in an otherwise sterile living room. They sat in the fort with flashlights swapping ghost stories, and it started getting too hot under the blankets, but they were too scared to leave, so they shed their clothes until they were all naked. But still, it was tender and sweet. The way one woman brushed her hand across another woman's shoulder as they laughed, or how two of them jumped into each other's arms as the story told by the third got to its spooky climax. Every minute or two, there would be a moment where one of the women would look at the camera and start to crack a smile, not as part of the scene, but as a young woman aware of her existence in this absurd exercise. It was moving. Each woman had a turn telling a story, and the last story was about a crime that had happened fifty years ago, in the very same house they were in that night. In the story, three women, just like themselves, were enjoying each other's company in the living room, when they heard a sound from outside the house. At first, they dismissed it. But soon, it returned. Slowly moving from one side of the house to the other, getting louder and louder with each thump against the walls or smack against the windows. Then, a masked intruder. Then, a second. The women in the story had nowhere to run. They were tied up and dragged away and no one ever heard from them again. The house was cleaned and sold and to that day, no one knew what had happened to the women or who the two intruders were.

As the story ended, the women in the blanket fort were interrupted by a single, distant thump. *What was that?* One of them asked. *I don't know!* Another thump. *Stop messing with us!* One of them yelped. *I'm not doing anything!* The storyteller replied. Even louder now, thump thump. The two women begged the third to stop, and the third woman begged the two to believe her. Thump thump thump. They all huddled together, flashlights ready as weapons, legs curled up to their chests, when suddenly from right on top of them–

BWAM

BWAM

BWAM

Their flashlights shot to the top of the fort and an imposing cock pointed directly at them through a hole in the sheets. They screamed in terror. The cock responded by wiggling around a big, like it was trying to say hello, then a pair of balls flopped down beside it. The women looked at each other and shrugged.

There was well over twenty minutes left in the video when this happened, presumably that's where all the sucking and fucking was, but Claire had never watched past this point. As far as she was concerned, that was the perfect end to the story.

Claire felt a soft kick against her thigh and was jolted back to the present. Tim was sitting on the bed, condom fully situated.

"Hey, so, do you, umm, want to…" Tim stammered.

"Yeah, sorry. Lay back." Claire tossed off her dress and stepped out of her underwear. Tim scooted forward on the bed. Claire straddled his hips, slipping him inside of her.

She started to ride, reaching back and resting her hands against his thighs. His legs were muscular and sturdy, like two bone-in hams waiting to be tenderized. A slow thrusting bobbed Claire up and down. Tim was a nice size. Plenty to work with, but not so much that she had to worry about any bad angles. He wasn't doing much, but that was better than doing too much. It was nice.

She sat straight and started working her hips. Tim's legs were confident, but his arms looked thoroughly confused. Flopped off to the side, palms up and motionless, like a mummy waiting to be embalmed. She grabbed his hands and placed them on her hips. His grip was soft and his elbows too straight, his arms moved up and down along with her body, somehow even more like a mummy than before, so she pushed off his hands and leaned forward. The pressure against her feeling better, better. It had been, what, two years since she had experienced anything but Ryan's wiry frame? His bones prodding out from his shoulders and ribs. Tim might not have a single bone in his body for all she knew, just a dense bag of flesh that would collapse if a few tendons snapped. The mass, the bulk. It was interesting, new. Claire grabbed his chest. His muscles reminded her of clay from the sculpture class she took last year. He was begging to be molded.

She pushed his chest downward, gathering him towards her, and could feel herself rising, rising. Once his chest was in place, Claire tried to flatten his stomach out towards the sides, but his abs were not as malleable. In class, the instructor told them that when clay was poorly behaved, they shouldn't hesitate to discipline it. It needed structure, direction. To hit the clay was not an act of anger, but an act of love. Claire pressed her fist into Tim's stomach. At first, just a push. Then another, then harder. The more force she used, the better it felt. Closer, closer. But the stomach still wouldn't budge, so she planted her left hand on his chest and began to punch down with her right. Strike, strike, strike. Almost, almost, almost…She brought her arm back behind her head and threw it down with all her force, but before it landed, Tim grabbed her wrist.

"Hey, umm, can you not?" He winced.

Claire sat back and felt Tim go deep inside her. Her legs started to quiver. She closed her eyes, inhaled through her nose, and grinded into Tim's lap as her muscles rippled and a wave of release washed over her body.

— — —

Laura checked her phone. Nothing. She had texted Claire like five times in the last hour and still no response. She was glad she went to school far away from her parents; if they wanted to dump any of their business onto her, they would have to wait till Thanksgiving break at least. For now, she had other matters to attend to. Laura swapped her phone for a lint roller and walked back to the bed.

After Mo and Lyle left for the party, Laura had stripped the top sheet and comforter off the bed and began to roll. They always made sure not to leave a mess, but it was the hair that was always trying to betray them. Mo shed like a dog, and if Claire saw the short hairs in their bed, she would know something was up. So Laura rolled and rolled and rolled and rolled, and when there was not a short hair in sight, she grabbed the sheets and made the bed nicely. But not too nicely. Then, for her pièce de résistance, Laura grabbed Claire's hair brush from her dresser and pulled out a few strands to sprinkle around her pillow. She plucked a few hairs from her own head to do the same for her side. Laura was a stickler for details.

As she was returning the lint roller to the closet, Laura's phone began to bleep-bloop. She snatched it up. It was Claire, finally.

"Claire baby, where have you been?!"

"Sorry, I ran into some friends from high school downtown and went to a club with them for a second."

"A club? Is this Claire Fost I'm speaking with?"

"I know, I know, but he had a whole rhyme about it."

"What?"

"Sorry."

"How was dinner with your dad?"

"Ugh, I'll tell you about it later."

"That bad?"

"Yes and No."

"Poor baby. You know what will make you feel better?"

"Reliving my recent breakup?"

"Watching the best DJ on campus get the party going!"

"I'm in a car on my way back to campus now."

"Perfect, see you soon baby!"

Laura gave the covers of the bed one last ruffle, then bounced downstairs to the kitchen so she could have drinks ready for when Claire arrived.

— — —

Mo unpacked his computer and mixer, setting up in the DJ booth carved into the back of the dance floor. He was excited to get into character. Sometimes he was DJ Midnight; dressing in all black, teasing his hair, and playing goth and emo mixed with trap beats. When he DJ'd kids parties, he was DJ Okey-Dokey-Artichokey; barely able to reach the turntables around his bulbous artichoke costume while he spun songs from kids TV shows and bubblegum pop tracks. But tonight, he was DJ Salt Lake Kitty. A Mormon cat with the slickest paws west of the Mississippi. Nine lives, nine wives. Baby, you know what it is.

Once all the equipment was set, he took out a compact mirror and some mascara that he swiped from Laura's bathroom and drew whiskers on his face. Gently, gently, making sure the angle and the fluff was just right. While he was putting on the final touches, a flash of neon behind the compact caught his eye. He looked up, and for a split second, saw Lyle's jacket weaving through the crowd. But then, it was gone. Disappeared into thin air. Maybe he was just seeing things. The crowd was grooving to the playlist the Beta House put on in between DJ sets, most of them wouldn't even notice that when he took over.

A Beta Bro approached the booth. "You ready to start?"

"Yeah yeahyeah, ready ready."

"Great. You're DJ I'm Too Old For This Shit, right?"

"Sometimes. Tonight I'm DJ Salt Lake Kitty."

"Whatever, we'll cut the playlist after this song. All you from there."

The Beta Bro walked away, and once the song faded out, Mo purred into his microphone and started spinning.

———

Laura was sitting on the front porch, hands resting on her lap, when Claire arrived. As soon as the car pulled up to the curb, Laura jumped down and wrapped Claire in a big hug before she could even get both feet on the sidewalk.

"Claire baby, I missed you!"

Claire knew she was trying to butter her up, but she couldn't resist her manic kindness. Laura was not a naturally nice person, she was sweet and caring and a great friend, but whenever she wanted Claire to go somewhere with her or do her a favor, she turned mechanical, like a robot who speed-read a book on how to be a human. Laura ushered her into the living room where drinks were waiting on the table. The pillows on the couch had been fluffed and arranged far neater than usual.

"How was dinner?"

"It was this whole thing. I don't really want to talk about it right now."

"I'm sorry."

"It's okay. How's your night been?"

"Good! Mo just started his set, you're still coming with me, right?"

"Uhhh…"

"It will be fun! Don't worry about Ryan, if he so much as looks at you, I will punch him right in his dickandball."

"That's very kind of you Laura."

"Anything for you, Claire. But we must hurry. Mo is all alone because Lyle has been running around all night losing his mind because he can't find his coat."

Claire was not surprised, Lyle was obsessed with that jacket. She was there when he started his love affair with it even. A few weeks ago, after Claire had moved in, she had run into Lyle one Saturday afternoon in the city. He was going to a thrift store and invited her to join him. She had some time to kill, so she tagged along. They had hung out at the house with Laura and Mo, but this was the first time they ever spent time together, just the two of them.

He had all these theories of thrift shopping, where to find the best pants, what electorics were worth trying to salvage, what makes a t-shirt perfectly ironic. They walked around the store, picking through the goods and laughing at the custom shirts that were only a thread away from being sent to the great donation box in the sky. Lyle put on some flannels, Claire tried on a pair of overalls that were big enough to fit two of her. It was nice, she was able to forget her existential dread and enjoy herself.

At one point, they had split up to wander. Claire was leafing through dresses and heard Lyle call out to her from behind. She turned around and he was wearing this garish windbreaker, black with neon stripes and these awful splotches of orange and pink. He asked her what she thought, and she was going to tell him the truth, but he was looking at her with these puppy-dog eyes and was so excited about the jacket that she didn't have the heart to break it to him. She told him he thought it was cool and Lyle's eyes lit up.

"Really?!"

"Yeah, very unique. It looks good on you."

"It's not too much?"

"It's a lot, but that's kind of the point, right?"

"Yeah, yeah, exactly. That's the point…so, should I get it?"

"If you like it."

"I do, I do like it. Okay. I'm going to get it."

"You should!"

"I will. I will get it. Are you going to get those overalls? They looked, uh, they looked cool on you."

"I don't think so, they're like ten sizes too big."

"Oh yeah, Of course."

On the train ride home, Lyle held the jacket close to his chest, crossing both arms over it like it was going to run away if he didn't hold it tight enough. When they got back to the house, he went straight to the basement to wash the jacket twice in the laundry machine (another one of his thrift store rules). He wore it every day for the next week.

Claire had only taken a few sips by the time Laura finished her drink. After putting her cup down, she flashed Claire an angular smile and gently nudged Claire's drink towards her mouth.

"Hurry up baby, we have to get to Mo's set."

"We have to?"

"We have to."

"Just for the set, then we leave, right?"

"Exactly." Claire chugged the rest of her glass. "Good girl."

Laura stood up, took Claire by the arm, and pulled her out into the night.

— — —

Ryan reclined in a camping chair on the third-floor balcony of the Beta house. When Sabrina sat down next to him with their drinks, he took his cup with one hand and put the other around her shoulder. She planted a quick kiss on his cheek and all Ryan could think about was how hot she looked. Like crazy hot. He first saw her two weeks ago at orientation week for new athletes. She had transferred to Foxden to play volleyball and was so hot. He made one of his friends switch with him so he could be the team leader for her group. He saw her that night, out on campus with the rest of the volleyball team. She was extremely hot and had a great ass. He remembered thinking that when he saw her, that she was extremely hot and had a great ass. And now here she was, in his arms at his party. Practicing mindful thinking had finally paid off, he had manifested this into existence.

Sabrina pulled at the hem of the jacket he was wearing. "A bit much, no?"

"You don't like it?"

"No, it's cool, you just didn't have it on earlier."

"Gotta keep people guessing."

"Whatever."

Ryan leaned back and took a long slug of his beer. The party was going great; solid line outside, good music on the dancefloor, no cops in sight, the pledges still full of vim and vigor. And wouldn't you know it, there they were. Grunting up the stairs with the sofa, banging into the screen door. Sabrina stood to help them, but Ryan pulled her back down to the chair.

"Babe, how will they learn if we coddle them?"

Sabrina rolled her eyes and returned to her seat as the pledges navigated the sofa through the door and onto the balcony. They set it down and rested their hands on their knees. The chatter stopped and the other Beta Bros on the balcony looked over at Ryan. He nodded his head and they lifted the couch. Then, when he flicked his wrist, they heaved it over the railing.

BWAM

Everyone on the balcony cheered as it hit the ground. Ryan turned to the pledges. "Hop to, boys." The young men trudged back into the Beta House and down the stairs to retrieve the couch.

———

Lyle's evening had been profoundly unsuccessful. Here he was, late into the night, and he was no closer to finding his jacket than he was an hour ago. He had searched every room, hallway, and closet he could find, and still nothing but dead ends. First, there was the VIP room that he tried to get into, but was told that since he wasn't on the list he would need to answer three riddles. The riddles ended up being the doorman's homework, which Lyle was desperate enough to attempt, but sadly his Physics for Poets class did not prepare him for Thermodynamics. After that, he walked down some damp stairs to a basement, but what he found was a cage full of pledges banging their tin cups against the metal bars, muttering something about *alms for the pledges*. Next to them was a pile of onions with large bites taken out of them and a freshman who would later be described in a federal lawsuit as being "beclad in a flax-thread loincloth, blinded with darkened steampunk goggles, affixed to a wooden cross with duct tape and fuzzy-pink handcuffs, and covered in a mixture of hot sauce and a type of yogurt that's only produced in the Agdash district of Azerbaijan."

When he emerged from the basement, he ran into Geoff, a Beta Bro he took a class with a few semesters back, who told him he was stoked to see him because he needed a hand. Geoff led him up to the third floor where a pledge was stumbling up the hall like a zombie. Geoff said they had to get him to the hospital, and when Lyle asked if an ambulance was coming, Geoff laughed and told him that he meant the Beta Hospital. Geoff took the kid's arms and Lyle grabbed his legs, and with some difficulty, they carried him down to the pantry next to the kitchen, where another pledge dressed in a sexy nurse outfit sat behind a table of IV bags. Geoff assured him that the nurse on call tonight was pre-med and much smarter than he looks. Then, Geoff told him that he would help look for his coat, but first they had to go play a quick round of Tar Horse.

So that's how Lyle found himself standing with seven Beta Bros around an octagon table that was decorated with a picture of a horse dripping with tar. On their walk up, Lyle had asked several times what Tar Horse was and how to play, but Geoff just laughed and told him it was easier to explain once they got started.

The game began with everyone chugging a beer while the Beta Bro who was gamemaster read the opening proclamation. Lyle only caught bits and pieces of it between his own chugging and the sounds of the other Beta Bros gulping and shouting. All he learned was that someone would become the Tar Horse and it would either be a good thing or a bad thing. Right as he was down to his last few gulps, he was hit with a barrage of empty beer cans. Apparently, he was last to finish, and now he had to chug another while everyone else watched and chanted *giddyup giddyup giddyup cowboy, giddyup cowboy cowboy TAR HORSE.*

Then, the dice. The gamemaster took out a large pair of golden dice and passed them to the Beta Bro on his left, who blew on them and rolled a two-six. Everyone murmured in approval and the dice were passed again. Next roll, three-four. Everyone started shouting.

"That's a Tar Horse baby!"

"Tar Hooooooooooooooooooooooooorse!"

A bowl was slammed onto the table in front of the guy who just rolled, and a beer poured into it. The guy leaned down and began to lap it up.

"Drink that shit up Tar Horse!"

Lyle leaned over to Geoff to ask what was going on, but Geoff brushed him off. He was too busy shouting. As the one guy was still drinking, the next guy rolled and got double-fives. Now everyone started yelling about a Ketchup Pony, but this time it was angrier.

"Fuck you Ketchup Pony!"

"You sick sack of shit Ketchup Pony!"

"I wish you were glue, Ketchup Pony!"

Beers were shaken up and sprayed at the newly christened Ketchup Pony. He quickly snatched an unopened one and began to chug.

From what Lyle could tell, the basic rules were as such: If you rolled a seven, you became the Tar Horse. The Tar Horse has to drink beer out of a bowl. If you rolled doubles, you became the Ketchup Pony. The Ketchup Pony was hated, and also had to chug beer, but they could chug out of a bottle. People said very mean things to the Ketchup Pony. There were more rules that were less clear; dances people had to do, beers that had to be shotgunned, cups and bowls and spoons and forks scattered across the table. Lyle imagined that this was the kind of drinking game the Mad Hatter would have enjoyed back when he was crushing brews and ditching millinery classes at Wonderland U.

The dice made their way around the circle, by the time they reached Lyle, they were slick with light beer and backwash. On his first turn, he rolled a one-three and had to chug a beer while lying down as everyone chanted *Four on the floor! Four on the floor!* Then, the next round, he rolled a two-five and became the Tar Horse, lapping up beer from the bowl while Geoff rhythmically tapped his behind with a leather whip that he must have been saving for just that occasion.

He leaned over to Geoff after finishing the bowl, "Hey, how do you win this game?"
"What do you mean?"
"What is, like, the goal?"
"Lyle man, we play for the love of the game."
"So when does it end?"
"Dude, don't worry, we'll find your jacket. We just gotta play."

Geoff snatched the dice from his hand and rolled a five-four. Lyle thought about giving some excuse and trying to sneak out, but his best bet to find the jacket was to stick with Geoff. One more round, then he'd bug Geoff again.

The dice made their way around the table, and when it was Lyle's turn he rolled double-sixes. Ketchup Pony. The bros fixed their vitriol on Lyle.

"Eat shit Ketchup Pony!"

"You're the scum of the earth! Scum! Scum! Scum, I say!"

"I hope you die, Ketchup Pony!"

Lyle began to chug his beer and tried to hand the dice to Geoff, but he pushed them back. "Double-six Ketchup Pony rolls again, big boy."

Holding his beer with one hand, he tossed the dice back onto the table without even looking. When they settled, the group cheered.

"A double-dozen-Ketchup!"

Geoff slapped the beer out of Lyle's hand and pointed to the dice. Again, double sixes.

"You sick fuck, Lyle."

"What? What happens now?"

"Roll again, bitch."

The bros murmured to each other, and Lyle began to feel uneasy. He rolled. Six-six. The room fell silent.

"A Mustard Mustang."

"What the fuck."

Lyle turned to Geoff, who shrugged and pointed to the gamemaster who reached under the table and pulled out a glass, a bottle of whiskey, and a jar of mustard. He mixed a scoop of mustard with a pour of whiskey and slid the glass over to Lyle.

"Drink up Mustard Mustang."

Geoff pushed the glass into Lyle's hand. "You have to drink it."

"But I–"

"The rules are the rules."

Lyle looked around and could feel a drunken haze slowly wash over him. The mustard was slowly separating from the whiskey and settling at the bottom of the glass. It smelled gross. Just this one, Lyle thought, then he could get Geoff to leave with him. Real quick, down the hatch. He lifted the glass to his lips and shot back the concoction. The room went wild.

"He did it! He did it!"

"No way!"

"The Mustard Mustang!"

Everyone, that is, but one Beta Bro who kept a surly look on his face. He smacked the table.

"Who the fuck is this kid?"

"The Mustard Mustang!"

"No, I'm serious. Who this fuck is he? Who brought him here?"

"Geoff did, right"

"Yeah, I did, why?"

"Get him out of here."

Tension appeared in the room. He wasn't joking. The Beta Bro next to him tried to calm him down.

"Crix, yo, chill."

"No fucking way this kid comes in here and rolls Mustard Mustang in our faces. And now we're going to let him roll for a place in the Relish Ring?"

"That's Tar Horse, baby."

"Not tonight. Not at my table. Get him the fuck out of here."

Lyle noticed the gamemaster walking to one of the cabinets on the wall and returned with a massive jug of bright green relish. He slammed it down on the table.

"He rolls for Relish Ring."

"The fuck he does, Geoff, give me the dice."

Geoff wavered. The gamemaster pointed at Lyle, motioning for Geoff to give him the dice, but the livid Beta Bro, apparently named Crix, kept yelling.

"Geoff I swear to god, we've been trying to get in the Relish Ring for four years and you're going to let this dipshit waltz in and roll for it?! Do not give him the dice!"

"Give him the dice."

Geoff placed the dice into Lyle's hand. "Go ahead Lyle, roll."

Crix stepped towards Lyle. "Do not. Fucking. Roll." Geoff pointed at the table, Crix took another step. "Give me the dice."

Lyle could feel the mustard and whiskey sloshing around in his stomach. He did not feel well. He rolled the dice around in his hand, they felt smaller and smaller with each jostle. He looked down. Then, a shove. Crix lunged towards Lyle and reached for the dice. Geoff was able to get in his way and knock his arm sideways, but Crix's momentum carried him into Lyle, and as he stumbled to the side, the dice flew out of his hands, right onto the table. They bounced, then spun, then slid, and when they came to a rest, two sixes were showing.

The gamemaster reared his head back and shouted, "RELISH RI-IIIIIIIIIIIIIIIII–". He was cut short by a punch to the chest. The gamemaster, coughing from the punch, grabbed Crix's arm, still hanging from the follow-through, and pivoted hard, tossing him onto the table. The jar of relish crashed to the ground, shattering into a lake of green goo. Around the table, the guys grabbed for Crix to restrain him. Trying to avoid their reach, Crix rolled across the table and knocked it off balance. As it tipped towards Lyle, Geoff shoved him out of the way, and he tripped over his own legs and fell to the ground.

The mustard and whiskey started to bubble its way back up his throat, and the smell from the mess of relish that was dripping towards him swirled into his nostrils. Beer cans were flying across the room, the table slid across the slick floor, and three of the Beta Bros were wrestling Crix to the ground. Lyle felt two arms grab him under his shoulder. It was Geoff.

"Let's get you out of here buddy." He dragged Lyle through the relish and beer, around the fight, and into the hallway, leaning him up against the wall. "Sorry about all that." Geoff slipped back into the room and shut the door behind him.

Air, he needed air. Or water. He definitely needed water. He could feel his stomach convulse. He needed a bathroom. Now. Lyle pushed himself to his feet and wobbled down the hallway. Where was he?

Was there still a party going on? Why did this hallway not have any other doors?

He got to the end and took a turn, he was back at the top of the front steps. The party was still raging on below. He looked around, a line. A door with a bathroom sign on it. He barged in.

— — —

Claire and Laura walked arm-in-arm to the Beta House. Not a bad night to attend a shitty frat party, Claire thought. They walked past the line snaking from the front and Laura used her feminine mystique to convince the Beta Bro working the door to let them in. They could tell Mo was still DJ'ing by the growling and hissing they heard in rhythm with the music. The dance floor was packed. Couples grinding up on each other, solo dancers trying to impress anyone willing to look their direction, freshmen scavenging the dregs from abandoned red cups. Everything you could hope for. After a quick lap, they decided to wait for Mo to finish his set in a less repulsive atmosphere, and headed back to the foyer. As they exited the dance floor, out of the corner of her eye, Claire saw a flash of neon coming down the stairs. It was Ryan, wearing Lyle's jacket.

"No fucking way."

Laura perked up. "What?" Claire motioned towards the stairs. "Oh Claire, no."

"Of course he took Lyle's coat, what an asshole."

"Claire, let's just–"

"No. Lyle's been looking for that coat all night."

Laura reached for Claire's arm. "Baby are you–"

Claire brushed away her hand, walked over to Ryan, and jammed her finger into his chest. "Where'd you get that jacket?"

Ryan was startled. His eyes slowly made their way from her hand, up her arm, to her face. "Hey Claire. Fancy seeing you tonight." He sneered.

"That's not your jacket."

"You don't need to make an excuse to come talk to me Claire, it's not weird to still be working through your feelings."

"You took it from the coat pile, didn't you?"

"I'm very flattered, but you know I'm dating Sabrina now. You know her? She's new on the volleyball team."

"Give me the jacket. It's my friend's, and he's been looking for it all night."

"Claire, listen, I know this is a hard time for you. Forget the jacket, if you ever want to talk, I'm here for you." Ryan put his hand on Claire's shoulder and she snapped.

"Give me that fucking jacket!"

Claire raised her arm and chopped Ryan in the throat. As he stumbled back, she grabbed at the jacket's arms, trying to pull it off him. Ryan regained his balance and knocked her away.

"Claire, are you serious?"

He grabbed her arms and pushed them into her body. She struggled to get out, but he had leverage, and she couldn't get her arms free. Her elbows were trapped, they couldn't even bend. Her hands, helpless at her sides. She needed to get that jacket. His legs were spread wide, maybe if she could kick out his knees or stomp on his feet, she could get some space. Surprise was all she had, so she inched her foot over, getting closer to his leg, ready to make her move, but then – *BWAM* – Laura slid in on the knees of her jeans and punched Ryan right in his dickandballs. He keeled over in pain and Claire grabbed the back of the jacket, pulling it over his head from behind like a hockey player. By the time his arms came back to life, Claire had wrestled the jacket free.

"Give me that back, you bitch!"

Laura jumped to her feet. "Go go go!"

Some other Beta Bros had gathered in the foyer to watch the commotion, and they were blocking the front door, so Claire and Laura sprinted up the stairs. Ryan chased behind, and when they got to the top, the line for the bathroom slowed them down. Laura turned to Claire.

"Go to the bathroom, I'll get him away." Claire nodded and pushed through the line. Laura stepped in front of Ryan and held out her hand.

"Where are you going?"

"I'm going to get my jacket back you fucking idiot."

"No, you're not. Claire is in the restroom."

"Who cares."

Laura cleared her throat and turned to the crowd. "Excuse me everyone, this man right here is trying to follow my friend–" The crowd looked on, concerned.

"Shut up! Shut up!"

"Then back up, please."

"You fucking bitch. Where do you think she's going to go?" Laura shrugged. "She's not leaving the house with that jacket. You know that right?" Laura shrugged again. Ryan turned and stomped down the stairs over to the Beta Bros still blocking the front door.

Inside the restroom, Claire paced in front of the mirror. She texted Laura and got a quick reply saying that Ryan and his Beta Bros were by the front door, and one of them was hanging out on the stairs waiting for her to come out. Shit. She put the jacket on, one less thing to carry.

From one of the stalls, she could hear someone having a bad night. A dry heave, a spit, a flush. Gross. She looked around and found a cup near the sink that looked reasonably unused and washed it out. She filled it with water and knocked on the stall door.

"Hey, all good in there? Do you need some water?"

"Oh, uh, no thank you, I'm good." A familiar voice.

"Lyle? Is that you? It's me, Claire."

"Shit, umm, hi."

"You okay?"

"Actually, I could use some water."

"Got some right here for you. Open up."

Lyle unlocked the stall door and slowly pushed it open. His eyes lit up when he saw the jacket.

"Wait, what?" Did you–"

"Laura and I found it!"

"You didn't take it, did you?"

"No, some asshole Beta Bro did."

"How'd you get it back?"

"Laura and I can be very persuasive." Lyle took a sip from the glass and coughed hard. Claire patted his back. "So, rough night huh?"

"Yeah it's been a whole thing. I think I'm okay now though. I need some air." Lyle started walking towards the door, Claire grabbed his arm to stop him.

"Actually, we can't go out that door."

"Why?"

"Also a long story."

"So…"

Claire looked around. A window. She walked over and opened it up. There was a fifteen-foot drop to the ground, but as fate would have it, sitting on the lawn right below the bathroom window was a badly beaten up couch.

Claire turned to Lyle, "Shall we?"

"You sure we can't go out the door?"

Claire shook her head. "We cannot. Now here, you go first." Claire lifted Lyle's foot as he stepped through the window and sat on the sill. He looked back at Claire, then back at the couch, then back at Claire. She smiled, winked, and gave him the double thumbs up.

"One and a two and a–" Lyle pushed off and plopped down onto the couch. He looked up, Claire was sitting on the sill.

"Get out of the way you goof." Lyle stood up and when Claire bounced down onto the couch, he spotted her fall and helped her to her feet. "Nice couch," She quipped.

"Not bad."

"Here, let me text Laura real quick to let her know we're out."

"Mo's set is probably done by now."

"Oh good, she can help him with his stuff." Claire walked to the sidewalk, then turned. "You coming?"

"Where?"

"Home."

"Oh, yeah." Claire waited for Lyle to catch up, then they turned and headed up the street. The sidewalk was thin, only wide enough for two people. Dew was starting to form on the grass. "So wait, where'd you find my coat again?"

"How did you lose it? You basically live in that jacket."

"It's embarrassing."

"Yikes." A few dozen steps of silence.

"So, I don't want to be rude or anything, but can I have my jacket back?"

"No."

"But like, I'm serious."

"Like right now?"

"Well, not like *right* right now, but…"

"I think since I went through the trouble of finding it for you, I should at least be able to wear it for a few weeks."

"A few weeks!? How about a few days."

Claire laughed. "That's nothing!? Laura and I fought off like six or seven Beta Bros to get it back.

"Six or seven Beta Bros."

"It might have been eight."

"Two days."

"Ten days."

"Four days."

"Twelve days."

"You can't do that!"

"Do what?"

"Five days."

"Five days?"

"Five days."

"Okay, deal."

Claire put her hands in the jacket's pockets and bumped her shoulder into Lyle's. She laughed as he tried to keep his balance on the slippery grass.

Odds and Ends

Write and Wrong Cocktail Lounge Specials

Goodnight Moonshine

2 oz moonshine

6 oz chamomile tea

Garnish with a melatonin gummy

Serve with a warm chocolate chip cookie

One Flew Over the Soju's Nest

4 oz green grape soju

3 oz plain yogurt drink

3 oz lemon-lime soda

Garnish with a slice of lemon

Serve in a plastic tube, Go-Gurt style

The Wonderful Wizard of 40 oz

20 oz malt liquor

10 oz orange juice

10 oz ginger ale

Garnish with a maraschino cherry

Serve with courage, heart, and intelligence

James and the Giant Peach Soju
64 oz Peach Soju
Garnish with a whole, unsliced peach
Serve in a fishbowl with 8 straws

Finnegans Shake
riverrunn, past the bar and kitchen, from splash of prite to twist of
tae, glasses of mask brunk us one sake with a wink and lindy andy,
side the scraglly cag, cold and cod, nor a topsway to a frite and this to
that parhops a flow and lark and a tag
Garnish lind a cabber laf cort than as than ronk
Serve ineer stim ol stam ol steame sto

8

I Am Falling

From my desk, I can see one window. It faces southwest. During the summer, we lower the shades when the sun passes by and a dull glow spreads across all the cubicles. But in the doldrums of winter, when the sun peeks out from behind the clouds, my coworkers and I all gather in the light like a clutter of cats. It has been gloomy so far this week, the sky an endless stretch of gray, but today, the sun fought through the clouds and the temperature snuck up above freezing and the office was abuzz with small talk about the weather.

When I left, the sun warmed my face and I thought to myself that this would be the year I become a jogger. Sure, I've gone on jogs before. Even stumbled my way through a 5k when a friend asked me to participate in her childhood leukemia fundraising team and implied that if I didn't participate it would be equivalent to personally giving cancer to the children. But, I've never been *a jogger*. I never had the mental endurance. In the past I'd set off on a track and run for seven or eight minutes, then get bored and start to think to myself about how I don't *need* to keep running. I could just stop and enjoy the nice day and walk slowly along the path and breathe with leisure and there was really no reason to keep running. It wasn't like I was training for a marathon or trying to win the heart of a very fast woman or anything like that. So I would stop. And I would walk back home. And it would be a lovely walk. And I would be reminded of how much I enjoy walking and my running shoes would be tossed in the closet to collect dust.

But today was a new day. When I got back to my apartment, I dug my running shoes out of that closet, did some perfunctory stretches on my stoop, then put in my headphones and set off.

It was exhilarating. My legs were fresh and my spirits were high. I got to the post office and began to assess my next turn. I could run to the ocean and jog along the wharfs where 400 years ago, Puritans first descended upon this land. Or I could cut back south and run to the house where young Malcolm Little lived with his sister Ella, then trace his path to the Lindy Hop joints in the South End that are now tapas bars and boutique apothecaries. I could even head east and run past the Old Harbor Projects where Whitey Bulger and his gangster friends started their criminal careers, inspiring hundreds of gangsters and thousands of screenwriters. But before I could decide, my right foot caught the lip of a cracked square of sidewalk. My body lurched forward, my legs kicked back, and now I am falling.

There is freedom in falling. My agency has been stripped from me, my fate is sealed. I cannot fight gravity and the ground is inevitable. The burdens of choice are removed, I must embrace the fall.

The first time I fell was the first time I walked. I was only one year old, but I have been told the story enough that an imposter memory has formed in my mind. I can see the fall from outside my own body, like a ghost haunting my own past. My parents and I lived in an apartment with a wide, light-filled living room. There was an L-shaped couch that would later be the scene of uncountable foam-gun battles and pillow-jousting matches, but on that day, it served as a wall for my toddling. My parents lazed above as I scooted my butt around the floor. And then, without warning, I pulled myself up and began waddling towards the TV. My mother gasped and tossed her book across the room, jolting my father from his cat nap. They watched as I took four small steps, then lost my balance and started stumbling backwards. My arms flailed above my head and my father reached out to try to keep me upright, but when he grabbed my hand, my body fell to the carpet and my tiny little arm bone was yanked out of my tiny little shoulder socket.

I let out a piercing scream from the floor. My legs kicked ferociously, one arm thrashing, and the other dangling by my side. My mother yelled that they needed to get me to a hospital, so my father, aghast at what he had done, scooped me up and ran barefoot with me down the stairs, out the front door, and down the street four blocks to the neighborhood Urgent Care center. My mother grabbed the first shoes she could find and followed him out the door, the slippers slapping the cement with every step.

When my father got to the Urgent Care center, he was histrionic. A nurse had to come out from behind the desk to calm him down. My mother arrived one minute later, just in time to watch the nurse take my hand, pull down and then out, and snap my arm back into my shoulder like a fleshy rubberband. Tears were streaming out of my father's eyes and he was blubbering gratitude through his runny nose. Once my arm was set back into place, my shrieks turned to laughter and my mother lifted me out of my father's arms. She embraced me tight and my father hugged my mother with me in between. As his body pressed against mine, I reached out to his face, took a scoop of his snot, and placed it into his mouth.

And still, I am falling. My head has turned inward and I can see two postal workers outside the front door pause their conversation to watch me tumble. One of them is older, in their sixties, perhaps. They've probably been on the job for forty years, walking the same route and watching the city change before their eyes. Three-deckers built, then abandoned, then demolished, then built again. Liquor ads and welfare checks, car notes and dot-com magazines, they've seen it all. The other is younger. They look new to the force, wide-eyed and bushy tailed. Ready to join the next generation of patriots who will not be stayed by snow nor rain nor heat nor gloom of night when there is mail to be delivered. When I reach the ground, I'm sure they will shout out to me to make sure I am okay. These two public servants, authorized by the United States Constitution to establish Post Offices and Post Roads, still have the kindness to care about a humble citizen like myself. The Founding Fathers would be proud.

When I was eleven years old, I fell into a pile of dog shit. My mother had dropped me off at school, and like usual (weather permitting), I joined a game of football with the other boys. We would haphazardly make and adjust teams, playing until the bell rang and the principal herded us inside. On this day, I played receiver. On one the last play before the school bell rang, when the quarterback called *hike,* I slipped past my defender and the ball was flung my way. It was thrown behind me, so I tried to stop and change directions, but my legs got tied up and I crumpled to the ground. No one paid my fall much mind, but when I went to push myself up from this fall, I felt a warm pile sticking to the bottom of my leg. It was a fresh pile of shit. I was horrified. If anyone saw, I would be teased mercilessly. I was usually able to avoid the rage of the bullies, but with this on my leg, they would come for me. A foul target had been smeared upon my jeans.

I was still on the ground when the bell rang, the other boys all ran into the school building ahead of me. If I could clean my pants before class started, maybe no one would notice. So I limped into the building well behind the others and darted to the bathroom. I kicked off my shoes and ripped off my pants. Holding them in the sink, I hammered the push-faucets over and over. The five-second bursts of water slowly chipped away at the crusting shit on my jeans. I was able to clean off most of the large chunks, but a dark brown streak remained. Out, damn shit! Out! I yelled. But no matter how hard I scrubbed, the streak remained. Plus, it still smelled like shit.

Then, I had an idea. If I could only get rid of the smell, maybe I could get by. I would say it was just dirt. They would still tease me, but getting made fun of for *looking* like you had shit on your jeans would be less crushing than getting made fun of for *having* shit on your jeans. In my pocket, there was a solution. That year at my school, tiny bottles of mouthwash were all the rage. All of the cool kids would bring them to school, exchanging flavors and brands in the lunchroom like trading cards. Tiny little bottles like you would get as a sample at the pharmacy or at a hotel, in colors that ranged from windshield-wiper-fluid blue to nuclear-waste green to horror-movie red. My father's aversion to name brands meant that I never could trade with the cool kids, but I could at least be trend-adjacent with plastic vials that had my family dentist's name and phone number printed on the label. I dug the pale-blue Kippinger-Dental-branded mouthwash out of my pocket and started carefully dribbling it onto the stain and rubbing it into the fabric. After I went through half the bottle, I leaned down to take a sniff, and the shit smell had not dissipated, so I dumped more and more out until the bottle was empty. I dug around in my backpack until I found another bottle, then I started again. Pouring and rubbing, rubbing and sniffing, sniffing and pouring. I was so focused on my task that I didn't notice that the principal had entered the bathroom until she put her hand on my shoulder.

Ten minutes later, I arrived to class wearing the emergency sweatpants the school kept in the main office. The principal ushered me into the classroom and I spent the rest of the morning picking at the waistband, trying to get the drawstrings tight enough so that the pants wouldn't fall down when I played football at recess.

And still, I am falling. My body has passed the point of no return. There will be no last minute miracle of balance. I will meet the sidewalk. Below me, I can see the different cracks. The points at which the cement has contracted and expanded, pressing up against itself until a fissure opens in the grain, creating mini tectonic plates that will collide and crumple upward towards the sky. A sierra on every square.

I fell at a high school talent show. It was the end of freshman year and the school had organized a show where anyone could sign up and get three minutes on stage. The list was long with groups of friends doing dance routines and kids playing whatever musical instrument their parents encouraged them to learn. I signed up, and in the space where you were to put down your act, I wrote *comedy*.

In preparation, I watched hours of stand-up comedy videos on my parents computer. I studied the stories they told, the syntax of the setup and the landing of the punchline. I deduced that the formula for success was extremes. Tell the audience an outlandish story then hit them over the head with the punchline so ridiculous that they would have to laugh. All the comedians looked so natural when they performed, I didn't realize that they all had written and practiced and rewritten their acts hundreds of times. I thought they were just going with the flow. All I had prepared was a story about getting arrested by the school security officer who patrolled our hallways. When it was my turn, the theater teacher led me to the stage, and with her hand on my back, she wished me good luck. My name was called, the polite applause faded, and I walked onstage into the abyss.

With the mic in my hand, I began to ramble. My story was incoherent and my attempts at jokes drew nothing but blank stares. I could see my peers growing restless. As the sweat started to bead on my forehead, my social life flashed before my eyes. If this act failed, all the kids would make fun of me behind my back, and I would no longer be allowed to sit at the cool kids table at lunch time. They would scoff when I would try to sit with them and cast me away to the table where the nerds would gather and play their role-playing card game. I would have no choice but to join their game, which meant I would have to ask my parents to take me to the specialty store that sold decks of the role-playing cards, and when I came back to school with my new deck the nerds would mock my basic cards and lack of strategic knowledge, so I would have to work extra chores to make more money so I could go back to the story to buy more cards and one day I would get lucky and find a rare and powerful card in a pack and then when I came back to the lunch table I would earn their grudging respect and then I would slowly become fully enmeshed into their role-playing game which would extend at first to recess, but then to after-school and weekends, and then during the summer one of their parents would organize a camping trip and we would all cram our smelly adolecent bodies into their minivan and drive five hours to a state park where we would spend all weekend in costume acting out magical battles and during one of those battles I would run into the woods to hide and I would see another campground nearby and see some kids our age and they would see me and call out and I would have no choice but to step out of the woods and see that it was a group of the cool kids from our school who were also there camping and they would realize they knew me from school and point and laugh at my cape and cardboard sword and the girls would laugh and the boys would laugh and when school started back in the fall I would no longer even be able to look them in the eye, so deep would be my shame. I could not let that happen. So I fell.

In my bit, the security officer was arresting me for possession of a bag of chalkboard chalk and I shouted *And then it would be like!* Then I punched myself in the face and fell to the ground. The audience snapped to attention. A few people chuckled. I stood up and fell again, my body hitting the stage floor with a resounding thud. The theater teacher backstage winced, but the crowd was eating it up, so I couldn't stop. Again and again, up and down I went, acting out a scene of middle school police brutality. Each time my body fell to the floor, the laughs got louder and louder. They were on the edge of their seats as I staggered across the stage, grunting and shouting as the invisible security officer threw me around like a rag doll. I felt invincible, my body only felt more alive after every fall, and I would have gone on until I squeezed every ounce of laughter from the crowd. But eventually, as I lay spasming on the ground, the theater teacher walked out and told everyone to thank me for my comedic act. Applause roared from the crowd and they chanted my name as I limped off stage. Later, the school nurse asked if I wanted any ibuprofen for the bruises on my arms. I hadn't even noticed them.

And still, I am falling. I reach out both my arms to try and break my fall, but my left hand makes contact first and under the weight of my body it slips, flailing out to the side and pushing my body rightward, right onto my forearm. I'm able to twist my body towards the street. I will avoid face planting on the cement. This is good news. I can see the city bus picking up a passenger in front of the post office. I've waited at that stop many times. The bus would pick me up and take me through Jamaica Plain and Brookline to Allston, where she lived.

On that bus, I fell in love. We met at a backyard boogie hosted by one of my friends. They ran in tangent social circles, and when I told him I was going to go talk to her, he told me she was trouble. But she had these big doe eyes and an enchanting smile, so I ignored my friend and asked her out.

The next weekend, we met for lunch then walked around the Fens, discussing our survival plan for after society fell apart. We agreed to meet up in Lower Alston by the library and then follow the Charles River east. We figured it would be easier to commandeer a house in Wellesley than in Roxbury. After we had set base, we would gather the suburban families into a tribe and become their warlords, then build a big fort around the town and make periodic raids on the science labs of nearby colleges for defense supplies. We walked through the Rose Garden and kissed in front of the Vietnam War Veterans Memorial.

I felt like a neon sign, ionized by the new current running through my veins. I rode the bus to her apartment every weekend and we explored the city together, every new block was another place to call ours. One day in the fall, we went to the Museum of Fine Arts and saw an exhibit from a renowned sculptor. The big attraction was a piece made from a hundred and one bicycles that the artists had welded together into a massive cylinder, thirty feet wide and fifteen feet high. While I admired it from one spot, she slowly walked around the outside, her head craned up to the bicycles and her hands clasped behind her back. As she finished her first lap, I reached out to her and she softly held my hand without breaking stride. She kept walking and our hands stayed in contact until our arms could stretch no more, then she released and walked another lap. We stayed at the sculpture, her walking without pause, me standing in one place. Our hands touching for the brief moments she was within reach. On the bus ride home she wrapped her arms around my body and nuzzled her head into my shoulder. I leaned my head against hers and was overcome.

But summer turned to fall, and fall turned to winter, and she became restless. She thrived on passion and felt most comfortable when she was off-balance. I never wanted us to be askew. She asked why we never fought, I asked what there was to fight about. Whatever she wanted, I would give to her. I cared only for her to be happy and to love me. But she wanted to be challenged, and I was not challenging.

For her birthday, I decided to sew her a pillow in the shape of the state she had grown up in. I spent hours tracing and cutting and retracting and patching, then threading and sewing and stuffing and trimming. Two weeks before her birthday, we went out to dinner and she broke up with me right after our food came. She said she would give me some space and left without taking a bite. A few years later, I found the pillow at the back of my closet. It was lumpy and only vaguely resembled the shape of the state. She would have hated it.

For the next few months, I couldn't ride that bus without being haunted by heartbreak. But I found solace in the overwhelming indifference of the other passengers. My pain did not matter to them, they had their own that I could not see. We all rode together on the same bus, our lives intersecting for one fleeting commute, only to diverge when we left the bus, never to cross paths again.

And still, I am falling. Just last week, I was invited to a meeting with a bunch of my company's bigwigs about some project that they want my team to focus on. They herded us into the big conference room and sat me in a chair along the wall behind the people who actually got to sit at the table. The meeting was mostly for show, they made an effort to look like they were open to our input, but really we would be getting the same orders regardless of what was said. Halfway through, I had to take a call, so I tried to sneak out of the room un-noticed. But when I squeezed in front of another backbencher in the corner, I tripped on the chair in front of him and stumbled into the file cabinet on the wall. I crashed to the ground. The conversation in the room stopped and everyone turned to look as I sprang back to my feet. One of the cabinet drawers was slightly ajar and it caught my pant leg, leaving enough of a rip to expose my shin and a thin line of blood. Without anyone asking, I assured everyone I was okay, then sped out of the room.

Later in the day, my boss found me hiding in one of our tucked-away conference rooms. He told me I made a big impression on the higher-ups. After the meeting wrapped up, one of them was ask-ing around to find out who I was, and when he found my boss he asked if I could be placed on a new project he was working on. He said I seemed resilient.

So now, I am falling. But its end is nigh. My right shoulder hits the ground with a crunch and my twisting momentum torques my chest upward. My head snaps towards the ground, but I'm able to flex my neck and fight the whiplash. My skull only boops the sidewalk twice before coming to a rest. My right forearm is bleeding and my left knee is scraped badly. As I lay on my back, I can feel them both throbbing.

Here I am, on the sidewalk, at the mercy of the world. Every fall has damaged me, but the wounds anneal my spirit and every scar is a brushstroke on the canvas of my life. No, I will not continue this run. I am no longer in the mood. I will lay here for another minute or two, until I feel ready, then I will limp home and tend to my wounds. The universe did not want me to jog this jog today, and it used its wicked methods to thwart me. If another bus were to drive by at this moment, the passengers would see a man down. They would think me weak and clumsy, with no fight left. Good. Let them think that. When you've fallen, you see things from a new angle. Things no one upright can see. You can feel the vibrations of the ground and the breath of the soil. The heat pumping up from the earth's molten core, flowing alloys made from the same stardust that courses through our veins. Every day we are reborn. The universe is infinite and expanding. I signed up for a pottery class and it starts next week. So yes, I have fallen. But still, I rise.

Acknowledgements

With endless gratitude, I would like to thank my parents, Andrea and Curt, for raising me with love, kindness, humor, and just enough disagreement to keep things interesting. My brother and sister, Max and Anni, for their creative energy and encouragement. Bubbie, Zadie, Grandpa and Grandpa for their open hearts and caring homes. Arunima, Audrey, Daniel, Gus, Nancy, Steven, and Vatsala for their generosity. And of course, Katie, my love, for every day we spent together.

About the Author

Sam Zuckert is a municipal bureaucrat who lives in Chicago, Illinois. He is a member of the Boston Retirement System and the State Universities Retirement System of Illinois. His favorite French Horror director is Julia Ducournau, his favorite mathematician is Georg Cantor, and his least favorite mathematician is Leopold Kronecker. This is his first book.

keepitgoinglouderplease@gmail.com